BODIES OF WATER

V. H. LESLIE

BODIES OF WATER

CROMER

PUBLISHED BY SALT PUBLISHING 2016

2 4 6 8 10 9 7 5 3 1

First published in Great Britain in 2016 by
Salt Publishing Ltd
12 Norwich Road, Cromer, Norfolk NR27 0AX United Kingdom

www.saltpublishing.com

Salt Publishing Limited Reg. No. 5293401

A CIP catalogue record for this book is available from the British Library

ISBN 978 1 78463 071 3 (Paperback edition)
ISBN 978 1 78463 072 0 (Electronic edition)

Typeset in Neacademia by Salt Publishing

Printed and bound in Great Britain by Clays Ltd, St Ives plc

Salt Publishing Limited is committed to responsible forest management.
This book is made from Forest Stewardship Council™ certified paper.

For my mother, across the water.

BODIES OF WATER

1

Kirsten

SHE NEEDED TO be close to the water.

It was a realisation that had struck her almost forcibly as she'd stood in one of the part-renovated flats belonging to the Wakewater Apartments development, or what would become Wakewater Apartments, once the restoration and modernisation was complete. But Kirsten had hardly noticed the interior. It was the view that drew her interest, the kind of view that she'd never be able to afford closer to the heart of the city. There the Thames was engirdled by concrete and metal, homogenous tower blocks lining the water's edge, houseboats and converted barges crowding the surface like some ready fleet. The people there were stacked upon one another, tolerating such confined living in their need to be close to the river. They had their exclusive view, but so did everyone else who could afford it. The water wasn't able to meander by without being watched by the whole of London.

But here, the Thames was surrounded by hedgerows and fields. Kirsten had looked out at the river and only its glassy surface had stared back. The opposite bank wasn't teeming with buildings but edged with trees and brambles. It was hard to believe that this same water ran all the way to the centre of the city, to those dense, overcrowded pockets where life swarmed. It was a relief being at a distance from it all. Though her commute would be longer, here, the river was entirely hers.

It was easy to overlook everything else. The flat was in quite a run-down state, in a large Victorian building that had been equally neglected. The developers were only renovating this one wing, so just a handful of flats would be made available initially before the rest of the building was restored. The refurbished wing would act as a model for the rest of the development – a show home. Beneath her hardhat, Kirsten tried to imagine the space painted and decorated, furnished with her things. But she kept returning to the view. Perhaps she'd been landlocked for too long. She hadn't known that she'd missed the water so much.

The estate agent expected the flats to sell quickly, mostly off plan. Kirsten knew it was a sales ploy to impose this sense of urgency, but she really couldn't bear the idea of missing out on such a prospect, quite literally. She dismissed her usual caution, letting it drift out the window where it floated away down the river. She wasn't even put off by the fact there was, as yet, no fitted kitchen, or that the ceiling leaked in the bedroom. As the water splashed against her hardhat, it only seemed to drive the point home. She needed to be close to the water.

'It'll be water-tight by the time you move in,' the estate agent had assured her, the assumption being that she would move in. Perhaps this language of certainty was another sales technique, or maybe he had noticed that she kept walking away from him when he was talking, to gaze back out the window. Either way, Kirsten had secured the property later that day.

It was with a sense of apprehension that Kirsten made her way back along the drive towards Wakewater Apartments on the day of exchange, the keys to her new home sitting in the envelope on the dashboard. It had been months since that first decisive visit and though the estate agent had warned her that progress on the main building had stopped – due to some hold up with the planning office – she wasn't quite prepared for what she saw. The site, which had previously been filled with vehicles and JCBs was now deserted. There were no men carrying ladders or laying cables, the drive was free of building materials and Portacabins. Strangely, without this veneer of activity, the building looked sadly exposed – uneasy.

Yet, minus the scaffolding, Kirsten could see what an imposing building it must have been once. Hadn't the estate agent said it had been some kind of hospital? It was certainly big enough. Much bigger than she remembered, now that it wasn't dwarfed by workmen and upheaval. It still possessed whispers of its former glory: the grand front entrance, comprised of pediment and pilasters; the gothic-style tracery around the windows. It wasn't just its size that gave the impression of grandeur; it had a sense of integrity.

She drove around to the newly-renovated wing, parking in the recently-tarmaced space that was allocated to her. She felt better already. The west wing was much smaller and the façade was less ornate, more approachable, modernised with fresh paint and box privet. *Wakewater Apartments* was inscribed in blue lettering above the modest entrance.

But as Kirsten got out of the car, she realised that none of the other parking spaces were occupied. It was a weekday; the other residents would surely be at work. For a moment though, she wondered if she were alone here. It had never occurred to her that she might be the first one to move in. She looked up at Wakewater Apartments, a building that was essentially a mansion, encircled by its own stately grounds. She couldn't see beyond the trees that lined the drive. She hadn't considered quite how remote it was, and quite how unsettling it could be if there was no one else to share it with.

It was with a sense of relief that she heard the sound of an engine and turning she saw the removal van making its way up the drive. The prospect of a pair of heavy-set removal men, armed with all her belongings, made the place instantly less daunting. Kirsten made her way to the entrance and propped the door open before taking the stairs to the third floor. Outside her own front door she struggled with the lock; it would be new, the key freshly cut. It wasn't well worn with age like the older parts of the building. It was modern and rigid, unyielding, as if wanting to keep some of Wakewater's secrets all to itself. Hearing the removal men on the stairs, Kirsten redoubled her efforts and the lock finally gave way.

It was certainly a show home. Magnolia walls, polished wood floors, marble fire-surrounds. The fitted kitchen was top of the range; the new appliances gleamed. And there was still that extraordinary view: of the river making its way past her window, outside three of her windows, in fact. She could run from one room to another if she wanted to see its slow, winding progress.

As Kirsten watched the removal men fill the empty rooms with her things, she felt an enormous sense of relief. Buying a flat in such a dilapidated state had caused her no end of consternation, though it hadn't been the renovation but the river that had troubled her the most. What if that strange instinctive reaction she'd felt to it had gone? What if the curious lure of the water, the almost physical need to be in its proximity, had somehow evaporated? But watching the dark surface now, stood beside the window, she felt the same uncanny pull. She could almost feel the water washing over her, taking hold of her body and rocking her gently in its calming depths.

2

1871, Evelyn

EVELYN TRIED NOT to look at the water as the carriage made its way along the track beside the river. She looked instead out of the other window, at the trees and hedgerows, occasionally the odd dwelling. When she tired of the view, she stared at her gloves instead. She wanted to look at the water but she knew what she would see there. It was the cruellest of fates sending her here, to be so close to the river. If her father was capable of irony, this was a particularly fitting torture. But he was only guilty of insensitivity; Evelyn's feelings were inconsequential to him.

The carriage eventually left the river behind and made its way through a small village, before entering rather stately grounds. Evelyn cast an unguarded look out the window now, taking in the manicured lawns, a solitary gardener pushing a wheelbarrow, the copse of trees on the periphery. And she saw the striking immensity of Wakewater House in the distance, the place that was to be her home for the indefinite future. At least until the doctors convinced her father that she was well again.

Evelyn was greeted at the door by the housekeeper and directed in for refreshments while the groomsman took her bags to her room. It had been a long journey and though she'd fought her father with every logical and emotional objection she could muster about the prospect of coming to Wakewater House, now that she was here, she found herself strangely resigned to whatever lay in store. Perhaps a rest was exactly what she needed.

After her tea, the housekeeper invited her to meet the doctor. Evelyn would have preferred to see her room and unpack, but Dr Porter was keen to meet all of the guests at the first available opportunity.

'Patients, you mean?' Evelyn said, correcting the housekeeper, a stout, serious woman.

'Dr Porter likes to think of those he helps as guests, not patients.'

'In case he doesn't cure us?'

The housekeeper conceded a tight smile. 'If you'd care to follow me.'

Evelyn followed her through the winding passages, which were illuminated by the soft glow of gas lamps. The house was austere, severe looking, without a great deal of ornamentation or ostentation considering its size. It was soberly, stolid, as if it needed to be modest and unpretentious if it was going to be taken seriously as a place of medicine. The housekeeper paused outside a door and knocked. A voice beckoned from within and the housekeeper opened the door.

'Miss Byrne,' she announced.

'Yes,' a young man smiled, striding across the room. 'Delighted to meet you, Miss Byrne,' he said, taking her hand before inviting her to sit down.

Dr Porter resumed his seat behind his desk. Despite his whiskers and moustache giving him an air of maturity, Dr Porter seemed very young to be running such an establishment.

He was perhaps of a similar age to Evelyn herself. She'd never met a Water Doctor before. She wondered if their credentials were different to other medical men. Did these therapeutic trends promote those who couldn't practice other more serious branches of medicine? For all her father's flaws, she doubted he would have entrusted his only daughter to the care of a charlatan.

'Welcome to Wakewater House,' Dr Porter began, 'named after our conviction that only water can truly awaken the body and mind.'

'Can you guarantee that?'

'Well, when our guests adopt our procedures and are committed to getting better,' he replied earnestly, 'we've seen some excellent results.'

Evelyn smiled.

Dr Porter laughed, 'I see you're teasing me. Your father said that you might.' He held her father's letter in his hand as if for support. 'He says that you don't have much faith in the Water Cure?'

'I'm here, aren't I,' she replied, rather more defiantly than she intended.

If Dr Porter was offended by her tone, he didn't show it. 'Despite what you may have read about hydropathy, we run things a little differently here. It's not just baths and bland food.'

'I'm sure.'

'He also informs me that you have quite an active campaigning life?'

'Yes, I'm involved in rescue work.'

'A noble cause, I'm sure, but one that has undoubtedly taxed your body and mind.'

'I think little of my suffering compared to the plight of those poor souls selling their bodies for a shilling a time.'

Dr Porter shifted uncomfortably in his chair. 'Quite. Quite,' he replied in admonished tones. Regaining his composure, he placed the letter down. 'But if I may, it's crucial to be physically and mentally strong, if you're to help others.'

Now Evelyn shifted in her seat.

'Despite the rather...brutish tone of your father's letter,' he continued, looking at her squarely, 'perhaps he isn't wrong about you being worn down?'

Evelyn smiled; she hadn't expected to enlist an ally against her father. But she was suspicious of doctors as a rule; Dr Porter's eagerness to pass judgment on her father could merely be a way to gain her confidence. Perhaps originally he belonged to one of the more dangerous branches of medicine after all, that of the Mind Doctors.

'Let's get you fighting fit again so we can send you back out there.'

Evelyn took in Dr Porter's youthful energy, his capacity for optimism, and she was suddenly aware that Dr Porter's station in life was decidedly different to hers. Despite his fine suit and his fine whiskers, his mannerisms were too casual, as if they'd been rehearsed to give the impression of nonchalance. And had she detected a country edge to his accent? Here was a man who'd worked his way up in life. An educated man of small means. The best and worst of combinations. Best, because he had been taught to dream, and worst because he'd learnt that few, except the privileged, succeed. He had probably spent his whole life pitted against affluent men like her father.

'And I wasn't joking when I called this place humble,' he

continued. 'We employ a small staff as well as the medical team, though I'm sure Mrs Miller – the housekeeper – will endeavour to meet all your needs. It just might not be what you're used to.'

Evelyn dismissed the images of the brothels and poor houses she frequently visited, the London slums where she'd spend most of her time if she could.

'I'm sure I'll manage.'

'We'll discuss your treatment tomorrow. As for tonight, dinner is at seven, where you'll be able to meet the rest of the guests and my associate, Dr Cardew.'

Evelyn rose.

He reached out for her hand again and shook it firmly. 'I think the water will agree with you.'

3

Kirsten

KIRSTEN HAD MANAGED to clear a path through the boxes, but unpacking was a slow process. Every few minutes she was back at the window looking out over the river. She'd read somewhere that when the Thames used to freeze over, street traders would set up an impromptu fair on the ice. It became part of the winter festivities for families to amble out onto this strange platform, perhaps skating over its surface, singing carols and buying roasted chestnuts from red-cheeked vendors. How odd it must have been to walk upon the river, to have gained access to this temporary midway point between the banks on either side. Though they saw the river rush past in every other season, they trusted the ice to bear them up.

Watching the river's surface now - so still and calm - it hardly seemed capable of destruction. But when the ice broke all those years ago, it wasn't just the freezing water but the perilous undercurrents that cut short the lives of those who'd ventured too far into its domain. How many people had it dragged down as the ice gave way?

Kirsten turned away from the water and resumed unpacking. She would empty three boxes, no, five boxes, before she rewarded herself with another glimpse of the river. She recognised the need to curb this strange habit now or she'd spend her whole time watching the hours float by. She couldn't deny that it made her feel better, watching the water. She was filled with a strange sense of calm despite how turbulent the previous few months had been. She'd hardly given a thought to Lewis, to the solicitors, the home she'd left behind.

It seemed like a good place to have a hospital. The water was certainly restorative. She could imagine patients looking out over it, as she had done only a few moments ago, allowing the river to take their pain away. It was funny to think that Wakewater had once been full of people, those sick and well, when now there was only her. *There could be others*, she told herself. Since the removal men had gone, she tried not to think of the possibility that she was here in this huge building alone. The evening was drawing in, soon the other residents would be returning home from work and tomorrow she may even meet some of them.

Sat among the boxes, she watched as raindrops glanced the windowpane, sporadic at first before giving way to the downpour. It felt like a strange extension of the river, this extra water, trying to entice her to come and look out of the window. There she would see the river dancing and bobbing as the rain struck its surface. But instead she opened one of the boxes, pulling out its entrails perfunctorily. She'd packed in a hurry; there was hardly any order to the contents, despite her scribbled labels. Among the 'crockery' she found the locket Lewis had given her. She wished she had got rid of it but she'd always felt a strange obligation to keep sentimental things. She realised now that she should have buried it deeper, or kept all these keepsakes – the ruins of her relationship – in one place so they couldn't surprise her now. How many of the other boxes were loaded with similar tokens, ready to disrupt her peace?

She turned the locket over. She couldn't bring herself to read the inscription, but she allowed herself to feel the letters with her fingertips. Though he'd told her a hundred times how there would never be anyone but her, seeing it in writing was somehow much worse. Because here was the evidence that he had loved her. Here was the proof he was a liar.

She dropped the locket back into the box and made her way to the window. The view was hazy, distorted through the rain and the diminishing light. Kirsten wiped the condensation off the pane, needing clarity, needing to stem the memories that were threatening to come flooding back. And there beside the water she saw a woman.

Kirsten stared, peering between the gaps in the smeared glass. The woman was standing at the water's edge. She couldn't see her face at this distance but could make out her long, dark hair. In fact, it looked as if she were facing the water, standing very close to it, or could it be – *was she actually in the water?* Kirsten rubbed the glass. What a ludicrous notion. But the image of the woman wading out into the water fixed in her mind before a gust of wind pelted the rain against the window with such force that Kirsten recoiled. When she cleared the glass again, the woman was gone.

She watched the water for a while longer and when she was certain there was no one there she pulled the curtains, leaving damp fingerprints on the fabric. It was odd that someone could slip out of view so quickly – *had the woman sunk beneath the surface?* Kirsten dismissed the thought, annoyed at herself for even thinking it. The woman couldn't have been in the water at all; it had only appeared that way. The rain had tricked her and was mocking her still with its persistent patter against the pane. She shouldn't be so suspicious of everything. Here was the likelihood that she wasn't entirely alone at Wakewater. Perhaps she had glimpsed her first neighbour.

As if in reply, she heard the pipes somewhere in the building – above or below her she could hardly tell – lurch into life. Someone in one of the other flats was having a shower, or running a bath. Kirsten was reminded how old the building was: though the interior appeared modern enough, the water system was clearly comprised of the original pipe work. But Kirsten didn't mind the distant clanging, the singing sound the water made as it travelled through metal; she was just relieved to know that she wasn't alone anymore.

4

Evelyn

EVELYN HAD PUT on her gown of green taffeta. She hated dressing for dinner; she'd have preferred to remain in her day clothes. Since she'd begun working with the Rescue Society, she'd developed a loathing for beautiful things. Though the women of the Rescue Society dressed demurely when ministering to fallen women, at soirees and balls they would dress as garishly as any prostitute. It was all about taste. But Evelyn had spent too much time in the company of prostitutes to distinguish between the varying degrees of ostentation. To her mind, all showiness and flamboyance seemed excessive now, offensive even, especially for women of her class who had no need to garner male attention for economic gain.

Only the green taffeta dress had escaped the cull. It was Milly's favourite. She would touch the fabric tentatively, hungrily, as if the dress were made of emeralds and not merely the colour of them. Evelyn had let her wear it once and in the candlelight it had given Milly an almost aquatic quality, with her hair hanging loose over her shoulders, the sea-green skirt rustling as she walked, which she did awkwardly, as a mermaid might if suddenly finding herself standing upon human legs. Was that the first time she had called her Melusine, after that mythical serpent-siren who haunted rivers and springs? Milly had never heard of Melusine, but she listened eagerly, as she did to all Evelyn's stories, grateful for everything Evelyn gave her, including that short time playing dress up, pretending to belong to a different world.

Evelyn hadn't expected this surge of feeling over a silly green dress and she turned at the bedroom door, considering changing into something else. But her eyes were drawn to the cast iron bathtub in the corner of the room and with it the reminder of her impending immersion into Wakewater's philosophy, of consenting to its treatments and therapies. She reached for her shawl and gloves with haste and opened the door, almost colliding with a large woman walking past at speed.

'Oh, I'm so sorry,' the woman said, seeing Evelyn start.

'Not at all.'

'I'm always running late,' the woman confided as Evelyn fell in step beside her, 'and I thought what a dreadful impression I'd make on the new guests. You must be one of the new arrivals yourself?'

'Yes, I'm Miss Byrne,' Evelyn said, attempting to offer her hand as they negotiated the stairs, 'and you needn't worry about bad impressions since I'm late myself.'

The woman stopped to take Evelyn's hand, 'How rude of me. I'm Mrs Goddard.' Mrs Goddard was a portly, middle-aged woman. Despite her cheerful demeanour, there was something formidable about her. Perhaps it was her attire: the severe cut of her dress, the starched material and the elaborate jet necklace that seemed to resemble chain mail. She was the kind of woman you would not want to make an enemy of.

'So you've come to join our little asylum,' Mrs Goddard said as they continued their way down the stairs. Evelyn was grateful to follow Mrs Goddard through the labyrinthine passages of the house. She wondered how she would have ever found her way on her own.

'I didn't realise I was in the company of lunatics,' Evelyn smiled back.

'Certainly. It must be a mad place when the doctors in charge want to dunk us like witches to see if we float.'

They approached what appeared to be a grand hall. It was better lit than elsewhere in the house, suffused with candlelight, a fire roaring on the hearth. Evelyn could see a group of people sitting down around a table. But not as many people as she expected, not for a house of such size.

'Are we mad too then,' Evelyn asked, 'for being such willing victims?'

Mrs Goddard gave her a knowing glance. 'Of course we're mad, dear, we're women.'

'Ah, ladies,' she heard Dr Porter say, approaching, 'we're about to eat.'

The table was set rather simply and Evelyn took her seat alongside Mrs Goddard. There was a range of women assembled around the table, some dressed more formally than others, as well as another man she took to be Dr Porter's associate, Dr Cardew. She imagined it was the newcomers like herself who'd come decked in all their finery. She'd heard that many Water Cure establishments favoured a more relaxed approach to dress, freeing their patients from the obligation of wearing corsets and stays. She smoothed her green dress, imagining herself liberated from it and the whalebones underneath.

'Dear ladies,' Dr Porter said, standing. 'Dr Cardew and I

would like to welcome our new guests to Wakewater House. We trust that you will find physical and spiritual calm within our walls and in the presence of that great river that flows outside our doors. Water, the purest restorative in history, has so often been overlooked by science, as being too simple to be of interest to medical men, and too ordinary to have a significant impact on a person's well being. I see it as a great fortune to live in an age of such vast progression that we can still recognise the power of the simplest of things. Because harnessed in the right way, water possesses the most powerful healing properties of all. Trust in it, and, I assure you, you will be cured.'

There was rapturous applause from around the table. Evelyn wondered how often Dr Porter had used that speech and if the existing guests had heard it before. None of the women seemed anything but captivated and she wondered if it wasn't the power of water, but the young ardent doctor they were actually praising.

'Please,' he said modestly.

The applause died down and the doctor signalled to Mrs Miller – the housekeeper – to fill everyone's glass.

'In the spirit of water,' he said continuing, 'Wakewater House is a simple establishment. There are no pretensions here. Simple routines, simple food and of course,' he held up his glass, the clear liquid sluicing inside. Evelyn reached for hers and joined the others in a toast.

'To water. May it restore and revive you back to health.'

'To water,' the room chorused.

Evelyn sipped her water, wishing it were wine, anything stronger to weaken Dr Porter's fervour.

The guests resumed their seats and Mrs Miller began to

serve dinner. Across from her, Evelyn regarded Dr Porter's associate, Dr Cardew. He was clearly the silent partner in this enterprise. Older and not at all as dashing as Dr Porter, with a rather severe aquiline bearing. Beside him sat a young woman with fair hair, appearing to be listening avidly to everything he was saying.

'When we think of how far we have come,' he said, 'not so many years ago, cholera was spread through the city by this very river we're getting so sentimental about now. It is a miracle of our age that our engineers have devised such extraordinary sanitary systems that the water isn't brown when we turn our taps. We should be raising our glasses to them and to the call for municipal waterworks to provide pure water for everyone.'

Evelyn couldn't make out the woman's reply, but Dr Cardew smiled and nodded. She imagined the doctors relished having such a captivated female audience. She read about mixed gendered Water Cure establishments and she wondered why Dr Porter and Dr Cardew had opted only to treat female patients. Did they think women were more susceptible to illness and malady? She looked around the table at the other female 'guests'. Perhaps they all suffered from similar complaints.

Reaching for her glass, the fair woman caught her eye. She smiled and Evelyn smiled back.

After dinner, Dr Porter led them to the solarium for coffee. Evelyn had not seen the solarium before and despite Dr Porter's rhetoric about simplicity, the room was ostentatiously grand, decorated with excessively large chandeliers and boasting floor to ceiling windows, revealing a large balcony that ran the length of the room. It would be a wonderful place to sit when the weather was fine. In the diminishing light, the view wasn't half as good as it would be in the day, but she could still see the grey, wide expanse, edged by trees and hedgerows, and she could make out the river, sleek and black, winding its way into the distance. She moved away from the windows and stared instead at the dark recesses of the house.

She didn't hear the young fair woman approach.

'You don't care for the view?' she asked.

Evelyn scolded her lips on the coffee and placed it down. 'I think I've had quite enough of the water.'

'Haven't we all. And you haven't even begun your treatment yet. Wait till you're two weeks in, so thoroughly drenched that the water will seep into your dreams.'

Evelyn thought of her own dreams of the water; not the calming, restorative waters that lulled the Wakewater guests to sleep, she imagined. The water in her dreams was black and filthy.

Evelyn managed a smile, 'I'm Evelyn.'

'Mrs Arden,' the young woman replied, linking arms with Evelyn, 'but call me Blanche.'

Evelyn felt her cheeks flush at the sudden contact, though she was no stranger to the forward airs of prostitutes. She was surprised that Blanche was married. The ease with which she took her arm, that look across the dinner table, gave her the intimate air of a confidant. She wasn't closed off like a lot of married women she came into contact with.

'Dr Porter tells us that you are involved in rescue work.' Evelyn wondered if Dr Porter discussed all his guests so openly.

'Yes, I try to help fallen women into refuges. The ones who seem really reformed I procure work for as maids or servants.'

'In respectable houses?'

'Why, yes. So many of these women just need a chance in life.'

At some point during the conversation they'd begun to take a turn about the room. Evelyn could feel herself being steered back toward the river.

'You said you try to help. Are you not always successful?'

She could see the river now, a black shadow in the fading light.

'No. Not all fallen women want to be saved.'

'Why ever not? They have a chance at salvation and they turn it away?'

It was hard to explain to people who weren't familiar with that world. Some women had begun the life of prostitution so young they knew little else. Others were distrustful of the do-gooders with their moralising and bibles. Some were more practical: they knew they would never possess the refinement to work in a grand house, and that after the refuge they'd be trying to survive with what little skills they had. They could earn more lifting their skirts.

'I can't understand it,' Blanche continued, 'and with such a beautiful ministering angel at the helm.'

Evelyn felt colour rush to her cheeks. She didn't know what to say. She was used to the bawdy retorts in the back alleyways, but not to flattery. She wasn't under any illusions about her appearance. She was resigned to her plain looks, her unremarkable features.

'It's difficult indeed,' Evelyn began, deciding it better to ignore the compliment, 'but I'm one of many who feel that we need to tackle the source, as well as caring for the unfortunates who are swept up along the way.'

'The source?'

'The men.'

Blanche laughed. 'My dear, you'd have a finer time locking up all the women in London than getting men to change their ways.'

'But it needs to change.' Evelyn realised she'd taken a step back from Blanche, her voice louder. 'How many women do you think I have seen, beaten, diseased, ruined by men's licentiousness?'

Blanche looked about the room, clearly taken aback by Evelyn's outburst.

'And what are you ladies talking about?' Dr Porter had appeared behind her. Smiling as earnestly as he had at their first meeting.

'We were talking about the dangers of the city,' Blanche replied, having regained her composure.

'Rest assured, ladies. You're quite safe here. The river is our moat, you see,' he looked at the water and smiled, 'and Wakewater, your sanctuary.'

5

Kirsten

THE DAY WAS grey, the sky the colour of oyster with the river running slick below it. There was hardly any difference between them, as if the world around her existed only in one homogenous shade. She was used to grey. The city was comprised of man-made greys, the colour of concrete and metal so typical of large urban spaces. But it was more remarkable here, this natural grey that distended as far as the eye could see. The sense of saturation was more complete with the water and sky merged together. It was almost like standing at the foot of an almighty grey wave, watching it swell higher and higher until it obscured the light. There it would seem to pause a moment, perhaps a while, before it inevitably came crashing down.

Kirsten had left the flat and was making her way alongside the water. Wakewater House appeared just as grand from the riverside. There were so many windows from which to watch the water, though most of the glass panes appeared shattered or damaged. And up there, a curved conservatory, perched out over the water, a stately platform to make the most of the river views. There were even little waves in the masonry. The building had clearly been designed with the water in mind.

She approached the section of water where she'd seen the

woman the night before and a sudden disquieting feeling began to take hold of her. What if she actually had seen a woman in the water, what if she had actually witnessed a suicide, dismissing it on the grounds of poor visibility and absurdity. What if now there was the body of some poor woman floating down there in the river?

She left the path and scuffed down the bank. It was ridiculous thinking such things, but now that they'd entered her mind she knew she wouldn't have any peace until she'd looked into the water. The bank was slippery from the rain and overgrown with bracken, which she clutched at a couple to times to prevent herself from falling. Her shoes and the hem of her trousers became caked with mud within a few minutes. She hoped none of the other residents - if, in fact, there were any - could see her from their windows, watching her stumble along the muddy bank like a crazy person. She edged her way around a cluster of brambles and there, beside the water, was a woman.

Kirsten couldn't have seen her from the path because she was crouched over. Among the bracken she was hardly noticeable, a diminutive figure hunched over at the water's edge like one of the many bunches of wild flowers that dip their heads towards the surface. In her hand was a large stick, which she seemed to be using to prod the water, and Kirsten was reminded of a witch stirring a cauldron. At Kirsten's approach the figure turned and stood, letting the stick fall from her hand.

It wasn't the same woman Kirsten had seen from her window. This woman was older, with thin, greying hair. There was a sense that Kirsten had caught her doing something surreptitious, like a child caught playing with something it shouldn't. The woman looked to the river as if composing herself, and when she glanced back at Kirsten, the furtive air in her countenance had gone.

'You must be the young woman in apartment three,' she said flatly.

'Yes, I've just moved in.'

'I saw the light in the window last night. I live above you.' She moved towards her. 'My name's Manon.'

'What a relief,' Kirsten replied, holding out her hand. She regretted it instantly. Though Manon shook it lightly, Kirsten had the distinct impression Manon disliked personal contact. 'I thought that I was alone here.'

Manon glanced quickly at the water and began to make her way back up the bank.

'Are there any others?' Kirsten pressed, following behind.

'No, it's just us at Wakewater. At least for the time being.' She watched Manon look back at the water again; it was almost as if she were addressing the river instead of her.

'But I saw a woman here, last night,' Kirsten stopped.

'Oh?'

'I thought it might be another resident.'

'It's a public bridleway,' Manon said, pointing to a wooden signpost. Just a rambler, I imagine.'

Kirsten stared for a while longer at the spot where she had seen the woman before following Manon back up the bank. It seemed that Manon was intent on leading her away from the river.

'So, how long have you been here on your own?' Kirsten continued, catching up with her.

'A couple of months.'

'Hasn't it driven you crazy, being in such a big place?'

'There's a lot here to keep you occupied.'

'The river?'

'Yes, the river.'

Kirsten heard some birds cawing overhead; she could see their dark shadows in the reflection of the river. She was grasping for conversation, but Manon seemed closed off, reticent. Perhaps she'd been on her own for too long.

They walked in silence, moving further from the river. Manon led them through a small gate and into the courtyard. The river was now completely obscured by the stone façade of the main building. Manon placed her hands in her pockets and her shoulders seemed to relax.

'Do you know what this place was?' she asked.

'A hospital, the estate agent told me.'

'No, it wasn't a hospital. It was a hydropathy establishment.' Manon saw the confused look on Kirsten's face. 'A kind of retreat, a health resort,' she explained. She began walking along the path that edged the house. She stepped over a series of puddles with care. 'A place for administering the Water Cure. It was very popular in the nineteenth-century.'

'Water Cure?' Kirsten asked, following in her footsteps.

'It was a therapy that used water to heal all types of ailments, from physical to neurological complaints. The patients would be prescribed all manner of water treatments, from being wrapped in wet sheets and cold compresses, to taking an innumerable amount of baths. Soaked, drenched and saturated for a few months, drinking only water, exercising a little and eating simply, the Victorians couldn't get enough of it.'

'But how could that cure people?'

'You have to remember,' Manon said as she skirted another

puddle, 'that this was before the birth of modern medicine. More conventional drugs at the time included the use of mercury and arsenic. More people died from the treatments than their illnesses. In comparison, the Water Cure couldn't really do any harm. And considering what hygiene was like then, most people really did benefit from spending their days lolling about in the water. This was a time when most doctors believed that being a gentleman exempted them from washing their hands.'

'Disgusting,' Kirsten exclaimed. 'You seem to know a lot about it.'

'I'm interested in this place, what it once was.' She looked up at the building with an expression of awe, then made her way to a side entrance and, with a movement born of experience, nudged the door with her hip.

'What are you doing?' Kirsten asked, incredulous.

'I just want to show you something.'

'But this is breaking and entering.'

'Until the developers come back, we're the unofficial custodians of the place. It wouldn't do if squatters got in. Better that we check the place out from time to time.' And with that Manon produced a torch from her coat pocket. The interior was suddenly illuminated – a kitchen or scullery from the looks of it – and Kirsten's curiosity was similarly awoken. She found herself falling into step behind her.

'Watch yourself,' said Manon, shining the light on the old flagstones. 'It's just along this corridor. Wait till you see it.'

It was as if she'd stumbled into a dream world. When she woke that morning, Kirsten had only thought of the river, about walking beside its silent winding immensity. But now here she was, following a stranger through the vast and musty corridors of an old dilapidated house – a house probably deemed too dangerous for even the developers to tackle. Visions of the building crumbling down around her filled her mind and she made her way cautiously over the boards, ducking quickly beneath the exposed beams and the dusty chandeliers, half-expecting them to come tumbling down as if triggered by their intrusion.

'Keep up, dear,' she heard in the distance. 'Nothing to be afraid of, I've been here hundreds of times.'

The light disappeared around the bend and for a moment Kirsten was left in the darkness. There was a faint chemical smell, reminiscent of hospital wards, and beneath it the stronger odour of damp. She heard a splash beneath her feet and as she moved towards the light she could see a thin sheet of water pooling from the open door.

'Watch you don't slip,' Manon said as Kirsten entered the room.

It was surprisingly light compared to the dark passages they'd just been through. Though the bottom windows were boarded up, the top ones had been left untouched and light flooded in from above, sparkling against the reflective surfaces.

'Well, what do you think?'

Kirsten hardly knew what to make of it. In the centre of the room was an enormous ornamental fountain. Though now defunct, she could imagine how impressive it would have been in its day. Scattered around the room were mildewed couches, and what appeared to be smaller enclosures like dressing rooms were separated by panelling and the frayed remains of curtains. The room was flamboyantly lavish, despite its neglect. From the double-height ceiling hung an enormous chandelier and beneath it the dispersed remnants of a large mosaic. The rest of the walls were covered with intricately patterned Victorian tiles, finished off with mahogany wainscoting. It was an overwhelmingly decorative space, especially considering the austere appearance of the rest of the building she'd seen so far.

'It's a wonder so much of it has remained intact,' she said moving further into the room.

'The developers have been pretty unforthcoming about the history of Wakewater, though clearly it's been in private hands until fairly recently.'

'I wonder why there were no attempts to renovate it before?'

'Maybe there were.'

Kirsten wove her way deeper in the room, noticing a handful of smaller drinking fountains set in niches. She moved closer to the central fountain, ignoring the stagnant green water that filled the basin, marvelling instead at the intricate waves carved into the marble. It emitted a low gurgling sound and a bubble burst on the surface. Evelyn instinctively took a step back and sank ankle-deep into water.

'Sorry, I should have warned you,' Manon said as Kirsten edged her way slowly back to the periphery of the room.

Kirsten shrugged and began to wring the water from her trouser legs. 'Don't be silly, it's only a little water.'

6

Evelyn

'WHAT DO YOU think?'

Dr Porter was stood at the centre of large, light room, flanked by an impressive decorative fountain. Chandeliers glinted overhead, held aloft by sculptured mermaids and nereids. A mosaic on the far wall depicted Neptune with his trident riding a shell-clad chariot drawn by dolphins and seahorses. Even the tiling represented the water, their blue-green current broken up by the occasional piece of decorative seaweed. Staring at it for too long gave you the uncanny feeling of being underwater.

Evelyn wasn't sure what she made of it. She wasn't really sure of what she made of the whole morning with Dr Porter. What had begun as her consultation had turned into a guided tour of Wakewater. And she'd hardly spent any time in Dr Porter's office discussing her condition. After diagnosing her with nervous tension and prescribing a routine that excluding reading or intellectual stimulation of any kind, he seemed eager to relinquish his medical mantle and show her around.

'Only a few people have seen this room.' He went on, 'You'll be among the first of our guests to sample its splendour.'

'Well, it's very grand.' Evelyn smiled. It certainly was sumptuous. Like the solarium, it seemed at odds with the pared down décor of the rest of the house. Dr Cardew clearly provided the financial investment in this partnership; perhaps he was explicit about how Wakewater should be decorated. At dinner he had certainly talked a great deal about progress; perhaps Dr Porter's simple living wasn't to his liking. And this room certainly exhibited an expensive kind of taste. Clearly there were two personalities in conflict at Wakewater.

'Turkish baths are quite the rage right now,' Dr Porter continued. 'This is the cooling room, where you can relax after your treatments.'

Evelyn looked around at the room, at the private enclosures where you could recline on couches, gazing up at the bright sky. Or sit beside the fountain, watching the water cascading incessantly into the wave-rimmed pool. But it was far from relaxing, with the sound of the water disrupting your peace.

'We have many other innovations in the pipeline, so to speak, that will undoubtedly set us apart from other Water Cure establishments.'

Evelyn murmured her approval and Dr Porter pushed on to show her the series of hot rooms, where she'd be gradually heated by degrees, before plunged into cold water. She tried not to think of the treatments as a kind of punishment. Dr Porter led her back out towards the fountain and, standing beneath Neptune, looked at her expectantly, perhaps slightly dejected that she wasn't more impressed by his vision.

'It's quite large,' she managed. 'Do you hope to expand?'

'Certainly. We need to share the miracle of water with everyone.'

Evelyn had wondered if he summoned his faith in the Water

Cure for the benefit of his guests and dinner speeches, but now she saw that he was a complete believer.

Dr Porter led her to back to the entrance. 'We'll begin your treatment this afternoon, so until then, why don't you enjoy the grounds.'

Dr Porter's passion was commendable, but Evelyn found herself relieved to be out of his company. She walked from the dark interior into the sunlight, then through the grounds that wound their way towards to the distant hills. She knew she was parallel with the river, but she had walked far enough inland that it was out of sight. When she felt a considerable distance from the house, she sat down on the grass.

It was quite overwhelming, this new place, these new people. Evelyn was used to being in charge of her own affairs, but here she was in the care of someone else, with a timetable and a routine devised without any of her say so. She lay back in the grass and considered how hard it is to give into someone's better judgement. What made Dr Porter's judgement better than hers anyway? That he was a qualified, that he was a man?

Evelyn wondered if that's how the women she tried to save felt about her. When she arrived at their door with a bible in her hand, passing judgement on how they should live their lives, did they think she was better than them, because she happened to be born in the right district of London, to a superior class, that she spoke and dressed with more refinement? She was certainly told so by indignant madams who felt they were the real ones looking out for the girls, giving them an income, a roof over their heads. It was a shame they had to work, of course, they would say, but every woman not born with a lady's privileges has to work, and the body is a commodity like everything else.

If they learnt the trade and were smart, they might one day ascend to owning an establishment of their very own.

But too many of them died along the way. Evelyn had seen her share of death in the London back streets and in the refuge where fallen women came to escape their former lives. The tragedy there was that these women wanted to relinquish their old ways, they wanted to make the climb back into civilised society. They'd listened to Evelyn's words and had realised how far they had fallen.

That was why there had to be more change. What was the point patching up the wounded, rescuing a few souls here and there – many of whom would return to their old ways when they ran out of money – when the most the world could offer them was life as a scullery maid. For the more ambitious and the more intelligent, perhaps being a brothel owner was a better prospect.

Evelyn sat up. She could see a figure walking towards her. A slim figure, with hair that glinted gold in the sun. It was Blanche, and Evelyn felt an anxious fluttering in her stomach. She shouldn't have spoken so passionately about her work the night before. She remembered Blanche laughing at her when she suggested men were the problem. It was the attitude she was all too used to. When the government declared that one in three men in the armed forces had venereal disease, what did they do to the men? Nothing. But any woman suspected of prostitution could be stopped by police and forced to an internal examination. Violated with speculums and medical equipment against their will. The Rescue Society had been very busy since that particular piece of legislation.

'Mrs Arden,' Evelyn said standing. 'How nice to see you.'

'Blanche, please.' She smiled back. 'So how drenched are you today? That's how you'll find you'll interact with the rest of us from now on. Conversations don't begin with the weather but how many volumes of water you've been submerged in.'

'You appear dry enough.'

'Oh no, when you come to Wakewater you have to accept your amphibious existence.' She reached for Evelyn's hand and brought it to her stomach. It was spongy beneath her touch.

'It's a water girdle. Neptune's girdle, though I don't know how I feel about the god of the sea sitting across my naval. Better to be named after his wife, don't you think.'

'Salacia.'

'Exactly. Salacia's girdle.'

'My goodness.' Evelyn's hand lingered on Blanche's waist. She seemed to incite physical contact between them.

'You'll find that all of us apparent land mammals are actually wearing the water upon us in one way or another. Hidden beneath our dresses or petticoats. Only at dinner can we take the damn things off.' Blanche linked arms with Evelyn as if they had known each other a long time and began walking across the field.

'I was thinking about your work with the Rescue Society,' Blanche continued.

'I'm sorry I was so forthright.'

'Not at all, it was exhilarating to hear you so impassioned. But I wanted to ask something.'

They had approached a copse of trees and they wove through the boughs single file.

'Of course.'

'What is a fallen woman like?'

'Why, they are just like us.'

'Evelyn!'

'What I mean to say is that they could be any of us in reduced circumstances.'

Blanche shook her head. 'I don't think so. Death would be kinder.'

Women of her class always thought so. They'd rather die a martyr's death than lose their virtue. In Evelyn's opinion, it was a privilege of the rich to place such a high price on virtue. When you are starving, when you have dependents, you'd do whatever is necessary to stay alive. Besides which, so many of these women were only girls when they fell in the first place. Forced into the life by circumstance, or tricked by seemingly benevolent matrons on their arrival into the capital. They could hardly be accountable for their actions at such a young age.

'Perhaps so.'

Evelyn ducked to avoid a cluster of crab apples. The trees had begun to gradually disperse revealing the river in the distance. Through the branches she could just make out a woman at the water's edge, a woman with long black hair.

She could feel Blanche moving behind her, flapping at the branches to move them aside.

'I'm entangled,' she called.

Evelyn turned to free her and when she turned back, the woman was gone.

7

Kirsten

KIRSTEN WOKE WITH the strange feeling of having been submerged. She felt relaxed, her limbs loose and warm, her skin supple and soft. She could almost fancy the tips of her fingertips were wrinkled. She got out of bed with a sense of lightness, an airy quality to her movements, akin to walking through water. Buoyed along the hallway and into the kitchen, she switched on the coffee machine with a numb detachment, a feeling not unlike having been in the water for too long.

The river must have seeped into her dreams. Wakewater was full to the brim with the water of the past. Kirsten could imagine the fountain gushing to life, whilst outside the Thames swelled and burgeoned. She remembered the cold shock of stepping into the water; her shoes and socks wet through.

The remembrance of her ruined shoes seemed to rouse her and she ambled towards the radiator she'd propped them against. They were still sodden and Kirsten realised she didn't feel much different herself. She was half-drowned, and it was no wonder considering the pressure she'd been under of late. She needed to break the surface, to stop languishing in the past and begin embracing this new chapter of her life here at Wakewater.

She sat down at her desk with a coffee. The boxes of paperwork and files were as confused as everything else, but she had to start somewhere. She couldn't rely on Lewis to manage her affairs any longer; she needed to learn to stand on her own two feet. She looked briefly at the river, at the welcoming calm it offered as it drifted past, before turning to the pile of paperwork with renewed conviction.

Not half as engrossing as the view but strangely absorbing in its own way, Kirsten became conscious of the sound of water. It was only when she finished scribbling her notes and sat back to read them that the faint sound of water dripping began to aggravate her. It seemed to grow louder with each repetition, forcing her up from behind her desk to discover its source. As she turned into the hallway it developed a percussive ringing, and approaching the bedroom, Kirsten saw at once what was making the sound.

The ceiling was leaking and each singular drip was smattering against the alarm clock.

'Shit!' Kirsten exclaimed, remembering the estate agent's promise that the apartment would be watertight. She climbed onto the bed and felt the ceiling. The flat magnolia expanse hardly gave anything away, but she could feel the damp patch and could see rivulets of water converging to one central point. So much for the estage agent's reassurances.

Kirsten pulled her cardigan over her pyjamas and put on her shoes. She made her way up the stairs to Manon's flat. Though it was a relief knowing there was someone else in the building, she would have preferred to avoid Manon for a few days. She wasn't quite sure what to make of her only neighbour. Manon was clearly intent on unearthing all of Wakewater's secrets, and though Kirsten was moderately curious, she didn't know how much she wanted to go snooping about the nooks and crannies of an old hydropathy establishment. She had a feeling Manon was the kind of person who would drag you along kicking and screaming.

The landing outside Manon's front door was crowded with boots and shoes, a host of umbrellas propped up against the wall. Kirsten imagined the developers objecting: it spoilt the modern, spacious feel of the place, but then, as the only resident for so long, perhaps she could do as she pleased.

Kirsten knocked and heard movement within. Was Manon talking to herself as she approached the door? It certainly sounded like it.

'Get back in there,' she said as she opened the door.

She'd directed the words over her shoulder, but Kirsten paused for a moment, wondering if she was addressing her. Then Manon looked at her directly, her reading glasses falling to the end of her nose.

'I'm really sorry to bother you so early,' Kirsten began, 'but I've discovered a leak in my bedroom. I wondered if I could take a look?'

'A leak?' Manon repeated.

'Yes.'

She opened the door wide. 'Take your shoes off first. I don't like to bring the outdoors in.'

Kirsten obliged and followed Manon into the flat. The place was crammed with books and piles of paper. Kirsten couldn't decide if it looked like a well-established mess or if she hadn't unpacked yet. But weaving through Manon's clutter, there was an impression of order, or at least of compulsion. They say that a hoarder's lair is the physical embodiment of that person's state of mind. If so, Manon's head was full to capacity, and spilling over.

The apartment was also unbearably warm, the heating probably on its highest setting. It didn't help with the place stuffed full of paper. A small tabby skirted out from behind a pile of newspapers and into the kitchen.

'Just ignore Sahara,' Manon said with a wave of the hand. 'We're fairly new acquaintances. She barely listens to a thing I say.'

At least that explained her talking to herself, Kirsten thought with relief.

'If the layout is the same,' Manon said, opening the door of her study, 'this room is above yours. I decided not to keep it as a master bedroom, I needed more space for my work.'

Space was an odd word to use, since she'd exhausted all sense of it. Though the room was edged with bookcases, they couldn't accommodate all Manon's books and papers, which had spilt out into piles on the floor. There was hardly any visible floor space and Kirsten didn't know how Manon negotiated her way through to the desk floating in the middle without sending it all tumbling.

'I'll just put the kettle on,' she heard Manon say as she withdrew to the kitchen.

Kirsten had imagined a bathroom being above her, maybe a kitchen or a laundry room. But Manon's study was an arid place of paper and books. Except for the radiator on the wall, there was no way for water to enter the room. She examined the radiator, but nothing seemed amiss and, edging her way into the room, she got down on her hands and knees. The carpet didn't appear damp. She had no idea about plumbing, but the water must have filtered through from somewhere else.

Manon returned with two cups of coffee, handing one across the gulf of paper.

'I'll have to call the developers,' Kirsten said, sitting down at the desk.

Manon sipped her drink thoughtfully. 'Sometimes these things have a way of clearing up on their own.'

Kirsten couldn't see how, but she smiled back. Placing her cup down, she saw that the desk was littered with images of reclining, naked women. Looking harder she saw that many of them had been dissected, their bodies opened up to expose their velvety red insides.

'Sorry, how morbid,' Manon said apologetically, sweeping them out of view. 'It's part of my research on Anatomical Venuses – life-size models of women made of wax. Medical students in the past would learn about the body, its internal structure, with the aid of these. They were incredibly detailed.' She handed an image to Kirsten. 'They'd have long hair, eyelashes, sometimes even pubic hair. They were quite beautiful.'

Kirsten looked harder at the picture. The wax model looked so real, reclining on silk cushions with its hair fanned out around it. There was something almost sexual about the pose.

'There's always been a fascination with depicting dead women,' Manon continued, 'whether for art or science. The nineteenth century especially was obsessed with paintings of dead prostitutes.' She handed over more images to demonstrate; mainly A4 reprints, pages ripped from books. Most of the women were depicted on sick beds or slabs – all naked. A few of the paintings included a male audience; medical men surrounding a seemingly sleeping beauty. In one painting, a piece of skin was being pulled back from the woman's breast as if it were a layer of cloth.

Kirsten's mouth was dry, she felt light-headed, her hands full of images of beautiful cadavers.

'Where did they find them, these...models?'

'Right here, dear, in the river. Do you know how many women were jumping into the Thames each week? Shamed, fallen women? Women who were pregnant or too poor to support themselves? You could just wait for the river to deposit them on the banks, nice and chilled for either the artist or surgeon. Both wanted to take a peek inside.'

Kirsten put the images down. 'There aren't any of men?'

'There were a few of what you'd call medical paintings, but not half as many as there were of women. It was a kind of voyeurism, I suppose; it was titillating for a predominantly male audience to see women so exposed.'

Manon's eyes seemed to sparkle as she spoke. In the light, Kirsten could see a fine smattering of downy hair along her chin and top lip.

'It was a time of demystifying women,' she went on, 'of trying to figure them out. And how do you do that? Why, place them on a slab and cut them open.'

Kirsten stood. The room was suddenly unbearably warm, overpoweringly so, this nest of paper and books threatening to smother her.

'Anyway, you didn't come here to discuss dead women,' Manon said, taking her arm. 'I hope you'll excuse an old academic getting carried away.'

'It's just rather warm,' Kirsten said, making her way to the door.

'To keep the damp away.' Manon leant in close. 'You need to dry it out.'

Kirsten wasn't sure if this was the most logical solution for a leak, but she nodded politely and thanked Manon for the coffee. Opening the front door, the cold air hit her like a wave. It seemed to sober her a little so that Manon's next comment seemed all the more surreal.

'Sometimes old places like this retain a bit of the past, in the fabric of the building, and occasionally, they seep.'

8

Evelyn

EVELYN WAS SITTING on the banks of the Thames. It was a warm spring day and people had flocked to the river to enjoy the fine weather. Women paraded past in the shade of their parasols, governesses pushed their charges in prams or chased behind them as they toddled in the long grass, and family groups stopped to fed the ducks at the water's edge. At Evelyn's side sat a young woman with dark hair. She had tied it up for this occasion; it made her look more refined that way. But the summer breeze had teased out a handful of tendrils which swayed lightly in the air like the dandelion heads along the hedgerows. Evelyn produced a brightly papered box from her pocket and slowly undid the ribbon that bound it together. Then she removed the lid, offering the contents to her companion.

'Milly?'

Milly smiled and fished inside. Turkish delight. She lifted a piece to her mouth, icing dusting her blouse. Evelyn watched fondly as she tutted and shook the fabric.

Milly had brushed up well away from the slums. Here, in the sunshine, by the river, she looked like any other respectable young woman. Except she was far more beautiful than most. In the sunlight her hair was so black it seemed to sparkle blue. Had she been born into Evelyn's class, she would've had suitors lined up. Even with a meagre dowry, Milly would not have struggled to secure a husband.

Milly was indeed a rare gem. Made all the more precious because of where Evelyn had found her. In an alleyway off Drury Lane. Hidden in the shadows, nursing a face that was the same blue-black colour of her hair. The gentleman client who'd had left her in that sorry state had decided to pay for her services with his fists instead of money. Evelyn had wrapped her cloak around her and walked her out of that life and straight to the refuge. She couldn't help but delight in the fact that she had found her, that she had been the one to hew her out of that rough earth and into the light.

And look how she sparkled now, sitting in the sunshine beside the river. Evelyn wasn't the only one to notice Milly's beauty. A couple of young men punting on the river had been casting surreptitious glances Milly's way for a while now. But Milly was oblivious to them, eating Turkish delight, watching the water. Evelyn often thought what a curse beauty was; that those in possession of it couldn't help that others were unwittingly drawn toward them. They had no choice in who they attracted. Even Evelyn, for all her intellectualising, wasn't immune to physical perfection. They were like beacons, shinning brightly in dark waters, unaware of how many ships flocked to their light.

Evelyn didn't delude herself that she was beautiful. She had a satisfactory bearing and had been fortunate to be born into a good family, where money and standing had given her more freedom than most women could expect. She sometimes mused over what it would be like if she and Milly were one person, if it were somehow possible to merge all of their qualities and virtues together. What a formidable woman they would make.

Milly edged closer to Evelyn. The fragrance of rose lingered on her breath.

'Tell me about Melusine.'

'But you've heard the story hundreds of times.'

'Tell me the bit about her being a serpent from the waist down.'

Ever since the first time Evelyn had affectionately called her Melusine, Milly could not get enough of the story of the water spirit who inhabited rivers and springs. Like most enchanted beings, Melusine couldn't help but make men fall in love with her. The story itself concerned a knight who, after chancing upon Melusine in a forest, begged her to become his bride. She agreed, but only on the condition that he would not enter her bedchamber on a Saturday. Folklore dictates that there is always a condition when a fey unites with a mortal. Of course, the knight didn't keep his promise and entered her chamber, only to discover her reclining in her bathtub with a monstrous serpent's tail where her legs should be.

The story is more about his transgression than about her deformity. Though she initially forgives her husband, when he exposes her secret in front of his court, Melusine transforms herself into a dragon and flies away, never to be seen again. In essence, it is a story about the need to keep a part of yourself back, that we all have a secret side we don't want others to see. It also suggests that the most beautiful are often afflicted with a monstrous side, which can be managed and tamed when they are alone and away from the world.

Milly had been wearing Evelyn's green dress the first time

she heard the story. The shimmering fabric had leant her a strange aquatic beauty. Mesmerising. Like the knight in the forest, Evelyn would have agreed to any of Milly's conditions on that particular night, had she made any. She wondered if Milly was troubled with her own dark secrets, perhaps she carried something monstrous around inside her too, something that she kept repressed and buried.

'Are there other women in the water?' Milly asked, leaning back on her elbows.

Evelyn ignored the obvious answer. Too many fallen women ended up in the river. Beneath Waterloo Bridge, the water swelled with drowned girls. It was better to focus on the mythical women who swam in the depths.

'Of course, there are rusalkas and nixies, sirens, undines.'

'No men?'

'Oh no, the water is a female domain.'

'That's good.' Milly smiled. Then she lay down in the grass and closed her eyes. Evelyn watched her for a few moments and then she lay down beside her.

9

Kirsten

KIRSTEN SAT AT her window with a mug of coffee. The evening was overcast and grey. The wind whistled past Wakewaker, stirring up the river, which seemed to possess a wildness she hadn't seen before. She couldn't help but think of what Manon had said about the river, about all the drowned women it had carried along in its current. There was never a shortage of corpses, Manon had said; the river was full to the brim with those who had no place in the real world.

The surface of the water seemed to grow more tumultuous under her scrutiny. She wondered if it had a sentience, the river, whether it was conscious of all the people that had fallen into its depths. Perhaps it was the sum of the people that perished in its depths. It made sense: how could it *not* absorb the life force of those who died within it. Kirsten had always nurtured a romantic idea that when someone died, their soul would float out of the body and up into heaven. But the water could make that tricky. Perhaps a soul wasn't strong enough to break the surface. Then, she supposed, it would have to linger beneath the water, occasionally aggravating the current into rippling waves and peaks as it was doing now.

She sipped her coffee and was glad to be inside in the warm.

Part of her wished Manon had not told her about the river. She wanted to feel that naïve awe again; she wanted to look on the river with only simple wonder. But Manon had marred it, talking about the past and its ghosts.

As if thinking about her was enough to summon her into being, Manon came into view beside the river. Kirsten instinctively drew back from the window but continued to watch. It was a particularly blustery evening to go walking beside the river, where it was muddy and wet.

Manon seemed dressed for such rigors. She had on high Wellington boots and a hooded anorak that she almost sank into against the ferocity of the wind. After casting a few furtive glances toward Wakewater House and, Kirsten assumed, towards her flat, Manon picked up a large stick from along the bridleway. Then she moved down the bank with ease, slipping behind the shrubs and briars and out of view.

What was she doing at the water's edge? Kirsten remembered the first time she had met her, when she'd been hunched beside the water, poking her stick into its depths. It seemed a strange, almost childish thing to do. Not at all what you would expect of a woman, she now realised, who knew quite a bit about quite a lot of things.

Kirsten moved away from the window and towards her bedroom. Manon had been right about the leak. After putting the heating on for half an hour or so, the dripping had stopped. She still planned to mention it to the developers, but for now it wasn't a problem she needed to deal with. She sat on her bed and pulled a book from her bedside table. Inside was one of the images Manon had showed her the previous day. She remembered Manon handing it to her and talking about it, before showing her countless others. It had been so hot in Manon's flat, so overwhelming, that she didn't realise she hadn't given it back until she was in her own flat. As much as she was loath to have it in her apartment, she couldn't face going back up the stairs for another encounter with Manon. She was resigned to returning it at a later date.

But looking at it now, it wasn't quite as repellent as she'd remembered. The image was produced on a glossy postcard, deemed tame enough to be sold in a museum gift shop. And the image itself looked as if it had been completed by a draughtsman; there was something very beautiful in the precision and detail of the composition. At the centre of the drawing, illuminated by an overhead lamp, was a beautiful dead woman. And crouching over her with a scalpel in hand, a man appeared to be drawing back the flesh of her breast. The image possessed a strangely clinical beauty; perhaps because it was black and white, devoid of the garish red vibrancy of blood and viscera.

Kirsten remembered what Manon had said about those pioneering medical men of the nineteenth century, that all they really wanted to do was to get up inside women's skirts and have a good old look around. Though the focus in the drawing appeared to be on the woman's torso, on a table in the foreground lay a section of skull and in the background an upright skeleton could be seen, depicted from the pelvis down. It was a powerful contrast to the beautiful corpse; a clear way to show what lies beneath our pretty flesh if the surgeons keep pulling back the layers.

At least this drawing wasn't as bad as Manon's images of Anatomical Venuses. There was something unsettling about those, something wrong about capturing a woman's likeness in wax. Kirsten didn't know why she objected more to this idea. Did it matter what medium the artist chose to replicate his sitter? But a drawing of a dead woman was only that – a drawing. You couldn't touch her and hold her hand, or if you had the inclination, to reach into her body and pull out her insides. That was what Kirsten found so disturbing: that you could interact with this work of art; a work of art that had been constructed from the wax mouldings of human parts.

Kirsten lay down on her bed. They were most likely the precursors to the life-size fetish dolls that had become so over-exposed in the media. At least the Anatomical Venuses had the pretext of being used for science. What did men find so repellent about real women that they preferred an imitation, anyway? Perhaps this was the natural conclusion when men seek to demystify women? They pull back the layers and find them wanting, realising that women are only human after all. So they decide to build their own version, like Pygmalion; an improved version, because their prototype doesn't talk back.

She rolled over and placed the postcard down. She didn't want to think this way about men. She didn't like the way her mind had started veering toward such negative stereotypes. But the end of her relationship had felt like being on that slab. She'd let Lewis cut her deeper each day with his words, and she'd allowed him to get under her skin. She may as well have run the knife through her flesh herself and peeled it back to allow him greater access to her heart. And he had rummaged around inside and had taken everything out, like the neat innards of a wax model, removing them parcel by parcel, until she was left hollow. Then, at her most vulnerable, he had walked away.

Maybe, she was to blame. If she were honest, she'd wanted to share all of herself with him, right down to the ugly depths. Isn't that what love is all about? This act of surrender, of opening yourself up and letting someone else in, even though there's no guarantee they'll like what they see. And sometimes they don't. Because it's the doll they really want. They don't want to spoil a beautiful package with human frailties and imperfections.

Kirsten curled into a ball and cried.

10

Evelyn

EVELYN LAY BESIDE the water. She'd spent most of the morning resembling a mummy wrapped in wet sheets, only to break from her chrysalis for a sitz bath, before breakfasting and now finding herself in the Turkish bath. She infinitely preferred the end of the treatment - lying on a couch in the cooling room - to all those hot rooms. Despite the sound of the fountain, she enjoyed the surroundings. The tiny mosaic tiles that made up Neptune and his entourage of sea creatures never failed to occupy her, and if she became bored with that view, she could always become lost in the watery wall tiles, wading between the wispy fronds of seaweed on the ocean bed.

A large woman, Mary, the water attendant, administered the procedures without much interaction. The Water Cure, Evelyn supposed, was about calm and introspection. If she wanted to talk about any of her treatments she could always speak to Dr Porter, but on the surface at least, things appeared to be going swimmingly. She did feel more relaxed, though she wondered if this was more about the break in her routine than anything to do with the magical properties of water. Besides which, she had her doubts about the doctor's prognosis. Nervous tension

– hysteria. It seemed too broad and vague. Perhaps it was right that it should be treated with a wishy-washy cure.

Everyone else at Wakewater seemed to regard the Water Cure with a kind of reverence. As if the water that gushed from the pipes was not merely the purified water from the Thames but holy water, each drop capable of healing its true believers. Mary had refined her job to a fine art; each treatment followed Dr Porter's strict instructions; the various baths drawn to his exact recommendations regarding temperature and volume. Some days Evelyn would be gradually chilled, on others she'd luxuriate in warm waters. Only Dr Porter knew what combination of cooling the body and inducing sweating would lead to her miraculous recovery. The only other person who seemed to see the absurdity of it all was Blanche.

It had become their habit to take a walk after lunch. They'd start at the house, then cross the fields toward the hills, then back down again towards the river. Sometimes they'd sit in the orchard among the fallen apples that were overripe and insect-ridden. Evelyn didn't mind being so close to the river. If she were sat among the trees she could hardly see it. She hadn't seen the figure by the water again – the woman at the water's edge with the long dark hair. She'd glimpsed her so briefly that she'd begun to think that she had imagined the whole thing.

Evelyn tried not to think about it, which was easy to do when you were in Blanche's company. Blanche filled the world so entirely, with her laughter and conversation, her easy demeanour. Evelyn couldn't help but find herself under her spell. She could feel herself opening up to her, confiding in her. They talked about everything: their treatments, the other guests,

Blanche's loveless marriage. They couldn't just talk about the damn water.

Sometimes Blanche would ask about her work with the Rescue Society. She wanted to know about the fallen women; not the ones who had seen the error of their ways and were on the path to redemption, but those who were enjoying their journey down to the bottom. What was the life of a prostitute like, how did they dress, wear their hair, conduct their business? What kind of men arrived at the brothel doors? She was curious about this world of vice that Evelyn had access to, hungry for all the shocking details. So Evelyn gave her the details. She'd tell her about the women she'd visited, bed-ridden with disease or from taking too many beatings, the ones who were marked out with the scabrous signs of pox. The young girls who flaunted their bodies like the older madams, their childhoods lost irrevocably.

Evelyn allowed her body to sink deeper into the couch. She wanted to forget about it, that world, at least while she lay gazing up at Neptune on his chariot. She looked past him to the higher windows where she could glimpse the sky. The clouds drifting by, and the sound of the water, gave the impression that she wasn't in the cooling room at all, but outside, floating along the river.

Blanche was different to a lot of women Evelyn came into contact with. Though she socialised with many of the Rescue Society ladies, there was always an agenda to their gatherings. They didn't have a lot in common besides their shared desire to help those less fortunate. Most of these women were rather matronly, with responsibilities at home; pious women who felt philanthropy was their Christian duty, though they probably relished the escape from their own marital obligations. Blanche, on the other hand, was young, vibrant, carefree. She was opinionated, open with her feelings and affections. And she was much more educated than the young women Evelyn saw on a more regular basis - the fallen women - whose company she enjoyed no less because of their situations in life. After all, it was inevitable that friendships would be built in the process of reform. But could she really, truly regard them as her equals?

Evelyn felt a heaviness in her limbs as if she were in the water and not lying upon a couch. The bathing dress she wore was far less restrictive than her normal clothes and she stretched her body, relishing the freedom of movement. She thought of Blanche, how she craved being in her presence, eager to receive the odd touch or caress she threw her way. Evelyn would never instigate any physical contact between them; she was too timid, too scared of rejection. It was Blanche who linked arms with her, who reached for her hand, or placed her arm around her waist as they walked. She was so free with her body, free of the constraints of how one should act. Evelyn liked that. She wished that she could feel similarly unshackled.

Evelyn was so lost in her thoughts she didn't notice that the fountain had stopped. It was only when she stretched again, leaning back heavily into the upholstery and hearing her movements so audibly that she realised there was no sound coming from the fountain.

'Mary?' she called hesitantly, wondering if the water had been stopped on purpose to signal the end of her time in the cooling room, the commencement of a new treatment. Her voice sounded diluted in the cavernous room. There was no reply, just the encroaching silence.

Evelyn pulled herself lazily from the couch and, looking up at the fountain, saw how eerily still the surface was without the cascade of water causing it to bubble and spit. She could appreciate now how large the basin was without all that excessive water. It would be quite easy to step inside and bend down into the cool water, to coil yourself around the central column, beneath those canopied tiers. You wouldn't be able to see the sky there, in that sliver of water.

Evelyn didn't know why, but the temptation to touch the cold, still water suddenly overcame her and she made her way slowly to the fountain and knelt beside it. The water was as cool as she hoped, her skin still retaining the heat from the hot rooms and hot baths that had constituted her morning. She traced her finger across the surface, thinking of Blanche and the orchard, her thoughts meandering away from the water and from Milly.

The shock of the pale hand emerging out of the water, the sensation of coldness as it clasped around Evelyn's wrist, made her jolt back instinctively. But the hand was strong and it pulled her towards the water. Off balance, Evelyn clutched at the marble border, her hands slipping against the ornamental waves as if they were rolling her down to the centre of the pool. Knowing that she couldn't avoid falling, Evelyn looked into the depths as if staring into a well, and saw the woman in the water gazing back at her.

Evelyn pulled against the current, looking away from that pale face encircled by that dark halo of hair, and thought how impossible it was, how improbable, though she could see the hand above the surface, the cold, hard fingers, digging into her skin.

Twisting against the momentum, Evelyn began to prise the hand off hers, leaning away from the pool with all her might. And suddenly she heard Mary panting across the room.

'Miss Byrne, did you call?'

The pale hand relinquished its grip and Evelyn fell hard against the tiles.

She heard the roar of the water first, before she saw Mary at her side, looking down at her with concern. Helping her upright, she stooped before the fountain, held up by Mary's strong arms, as water gushed and poured onto her.

11

Kirsten

KIRSTEN COULD FEEL the water. She could feel its cooling touch on her face and shoulders. The shiver of cold as it touched her neck. She was reclining into it, her body tilting back, expecting the river to support her. She spread out her arms and legs, stretching as much as she could, letting the water enjoy as much of her as possible. She opened her mouth and the water gushed in. She welcomed this feeling of immersion, of surrendering briefly to its influence.

But when she turned her head to clear her lungs, she couldn't seem to get rid of the water. Instead it felt as if there were more of it, that it was overpowering her. She began to sink beneath the surface, the water in her mouth and stomach, a lead weight dragging her down. She tried to expel the water, but every time she opened her mouth, more rushed in. She thrashed and flailed and she sank deeper.

She opened her eyes but still couldn't breathe. She was conscious of the familiar surroundings of her bedroom, but she felt as if she were still ingesting the river water. It was a dream, though she realised with alarm that somehow she couldn't get her breath. She sat up in bed and began to cough up what had found its way into her throat and lungs.

She keeled over exhausted. Water smattered against her head and she realised that the bed sheets were soaked. The leak must have begun again in the night, this time in earnest, almost drowning her as she slept.

She hauled herself out of bed and out of the range of the dripping water. She put on dry clothes and made her way to the door, cursing Manon for making her believe that she could magic this problem away. The water had to be coming from somewhere and she wouldn't leave Manon's flat until she had discovered its source.

She made her way up the flight of stairs and knocked heavily on Manon's door.

Almost instantly she heard a low scratching on the other side of the door. Sahara, Manon's cat. She knocked again. Still no answer, but the scratching seemed to double in intensity. Maybe Manon had gone out and had forgotten to feed her.

'There, there, Sahara,' she called through the door, 'Manon will be home soon.'

She gave one last knock and was about to walk away when she heard a distant call from within.

'Manon?'

She could hear it again. A soft, low call. Almost a plea.

'Manon, are you OK?'

There was no letterbox to look through, so Kirsten got down on her hands and knees and tried to peer beneath the door. She couldn't see much, but she could hear more clearly.

'Manon?' she called again.

This time she heard a reply.

'Kirsten, I've fallen.'

Kirsten straightened. 'Don't worry, Manon, I'll get help.'

She pulled herself off the floor and made her way back to her flat. It was only when she called the emergency services that she realised that her clothes were damp. The floor must've been wet as she crouched down outside Manon's door. Kirsten remembered the watery manner in which she'd woken; it seemed impossible to be dry at Wakewater.

It took two policemen to open Manon's door and then the paramedics filed in, one at a time, to negotiate Manon's clutter. Wakewater was unused to so much commotion. Kirsten wondered if it disliked this sudden surge of activity, that it was intolerant to anything other than the slow, steady progress of the river outside.

They found Manon in the bathroom. Lying against the tiles. She'd slipped, she told them. Kirsten waited by the front door; she didn't want to be in the way. But she could see part of the scene: Manon's legs, the paramedic's emergency bag resting on the wet floor, and occasionally the paramedics as they moved about, asking questions, checking Manon's vitals. She watched one of them prepare a syringe. Occasionally she could hear Manon speaking lowly to the paramedics.

'It's the water, you know, full of oestrogen. It's feminised the water.'

'There, there,' the paramedic replied, 'let's get you to the hospital.'

'That's what's done it,' she continued. 'It's stirred them all up. Brought them to the surface.'

Kirsten watched as Manon was placed on a spine board. The two policemen helped carry her over the pile of books and paperwork to the stairwell. As she passed Kirsten in the doorway, Manon reached out to her.

'Kirsten, dear, would you look after Sahara?'

'Of course.' Kirsten smiled. 'You needn't worry.'

Manon smiled back. And for a moment they really looked at each other. Then the calm was broken and an expression of desperation flooded Manon's features. She grabbed Kirsten's hand and held it tightly. 'If they try to come up, push them down again. Push them back down!'

12

Evelyn

THEY WERE SAT in the orchard among the fallen crab apples. Occasionally Blanche would pick one up and examine its yellow flesh as if she were about to take a bite. Then she would set it down again, knowing the fruit would be too sour. Evelyn hardly noticed; her mind was still in the cooling room with the strange vision in the water. The woman with the dark wet hair. She had been there, Evelyn was certain, she could still feel her grasp on her wrist; she had not conjured her out of vapour.

Since then, Evelyn could think of little else. She'd seen her once before, that day beside the river. Evelyn positioned herself now with her back to the Thames and could see instead the line of trees stretching towards the house and gardens. But it didn't make any difference because when she closed her eyes the woman was in her mind, her face just below the surface. Evelyn wanted to forget the water and this strange woman who resided there, but Wakewater's foundations were too immersed.

'You're quiet today,' Blanche said.

Evelyn managed a smile. Usually she delighted in Blanche's company, relishing her easy manner, their closeness, but today it felt so flimsy and insubstantial. They didn't know each other, not really. The only thing they had in common was being here at Wakewater.

'Would you like to know a secret?' Blanche asked, sidling closer.

Evelyn shrugged. She'd known respectable women and whores to trade in secrets, using the same luring tone. It was better to pretend you weren't interested. Usually the purveyor was desperate to give them away.

'I know what Dr Porter has in the basement.'

Though it piqued Evelyn's interest, she wasn't going to show it. 'I'm sure that whatever it is, it's fundamental to his research.'

'Evelyn!' Blanche said, dejected. 'Whatever is wrong with you?'

She could understand why Blanche was hurt. Evelyn had been a good audience until now. She'd listened to all of Blanche's gossip on the other patients. She knew all about their romantic histories, their thwarted love matches, the information they divulged to one another when they were relaxed and open from too many steam baths. However, it was the other things she somehow knew, things that Evelyn couldn't imagine her fellow patients readily disclosing. For instance, Mrs Bartholomew was at Wakewater because of a prolapsed uterus, Mrs Wilmot was being treated for bareness, and Mrs Goddard was recovering from a hysterectomy. Evelyn had been right about Wakewater's clientele. The women all came from the same pool. Evelyn and her hysteria fitted right in; Wakewater was a centre for women's 'complaints'.

If that wasn't evidence enough, Blanche had said she'd seen Dr Porter's obstetric and gynaecological instruments. They were concealed in a cabinet in his office. Evelyn hadn't questioned how she'd come to know this; she didn't want to encourage Blanche's gossip-mongering habit. But it was clear that Blanche had an insatiable curiosity. Evelyn could imagine her snooping around when the opportunity presented itself. At least it meant that Evelyn understood more about Dr Porter and which branch of medicine he belonged to.

'I'm sorry,' Evelyn managed, 'I haven't been myself.'

'That's why you are here,' Blanche replied earnestly, taking her hand, 'to return to yourself, to mend. And I believe I know what it is that you are really recovering from.'

Evelyn shifted under her gaze. She had tolerated Dr Porter's diagnosis, the treatments he'd devised to cure her, and she wasn't going to subject herself to further speculation.

'I know you think I'm a terrible gossip,' Blanche continued, 'sharing all these secrets with you. I can't keep secrets, I feel them bubbling up inside of me. But there's one thing I've never told you, I've never told a soul at Wakewater, besides the doctor,' she smiled releasing Evelyn's hand. Then she looked into the distance, toward the river.

'I lost a child. Almost a year ago now.' She began to smooth the fabric of her skirts. 'It was a horrific birth. The baby was already dead when they pulled her from me. It was a little girl, you see. A sickly, tiny thing. She wouldn't have lived long had she survived the birth.'

Blanche reached for the crab apple she'd been toying with earlier. She rolled it in her hands before placing it in her lap.

'Sometimes, I almost fancy I hear her crying. Which is ridiculous. My poor girl never had the breath to cry. She was born blue and silent. But sometimes, when I'm lying in the bath on doctor's orders, my head just below the surface, I swear I can hear wailing in the water. They say it's a mother's intuition to know the cry of your own child. I don't expect you to believe me, but I know without any doubt that it's my little girl calling me through the water.'

Evelyn looked at Blanche for what felt like a long time. Then she reached over and laid her hand against her stomach. Neptune's Girdle swaddled her waist, water encircling the place where her baby had died. It seemed so unfair, that women had been tasked with the weight of childbearing, cursed with this organ, which seemed to bring only pain to the bearer. Why would anyone choose such a burden?

'I think the sufferers of grief can recognise one another clearly enough,' Blanche continued. 'Perhaps it's having so much time here to think, to loll about in baths and steam rooms, letting our misery float to the surface. But I think that you've felt something in the water too.'

Evelyn stood and faced the river. There it swept by, grey and sombre, constant, primordial. Evelyn wasn't ready to share her secrets, but she wanted to give Blanche something in return. She held out her hands and lifted Blanche to her feet. And as the apple fell from her skirts, Evelyn pulled Blanche toward her and kissed her softly on the mouth.

13

Kirsten

KIRSTEN RAN A bath. It had been an eventful day and she felt exhausted. Outside it was raining hard and the patter against the windowpane seemed to provide an almost pleasing accompaniment to the water streaming from the taps. The weather had turned much colder. The forecasters were predicting ground frost. If it was severe enough the river, or at least patches of it, could ice over. Had it been a few days ago, Kirsten would have looked forward to this change, of adding it to her mental repository of the river and its shifting nature. But Manon's words had perplexed her, with all that talk of drowned girls and the water being stirred up. Though she barely understood what she meant, she couldn't help but look at the river in a different way. Perhaps there was something unnatural about it. She could feel her enchantment with it gradually ebbing away and in its place was something else, something like distrust.

Kirsten heard a purr and felt a wet lapping against her ankle. Sahara weaved herself between Kirsten's legs before sauntering off toward the radiator.

She didn't know why she listened to Manon. The paramedics had given her a shot; it was more likely the morphine talking. That, combined with the fact Manon had been living too long on her own at Wakewater, allowing her anxieties and delusions to get the better of her. With only her historical obsessions – her pictures of drowned prostitutes and a cat for company, was it any wonder she said some of the things she did? But now Manon had been taken away, having passed on her apprehension of the river, and now Kirsten was the sole resident of Wakewater.

But she wasn't alone.

Beside the river stood a woman with long dark hair. Kirsten hadn't seen her approach, the driving rain having made visibility difficult, but she could make her out now, vaguely, in the fading light. It looked like the same woman she'd seen that first night at Wakewater, the one she had told Manon about. But the woman stood at a different spot along the river. Closer to the house. And she wasn't looking towards the river as she had been before, but was staring up at Wakewater, towards the light that shone from Kirsten's window.

It was a public path, Kirsten told herself. It could be anyone out for an evening stroll. But there was something curious about the woman stood so motionless beside the water. The bank, and the briars that grew there in such abundance, obscured the lower part of her body, and Kirsten was struck again with the notion that the woman wasn't standing beside the river at all, but was standing *in* the water.

Though she knew the woman would be able to see her – the light of her apartment a beacon in the dusk – she continued to stare. She didn't want to break eye contact with this strange woman. She had the curious feeling that if she did, the woman would dissolve into nothingness, that she would be spirited into the water. She realised how ludicrous she sounded, how like Manon, but she couldn't shake the uncanny feeling that while she maintained sight of her, the woman *belonged* to the corporeal world. She was as real as the river.

From across the room, she heard a hiss, and turning unwillingly from her view of the woman, saw Sahara stretched tall, her fur standing on end. Her scant body was facing the bathroom and slowly backing away from the water that pooled out into the hallway.

Kirsten rushed toward the bathroom, slowing down as quickly to negotiate the wet floor. Was this how Manon fell? How long had she been watching the strange woman by the river for the bathwater to overflow? She walked cautiously across the tiles and leant across to turn off the taps. She watched the water spiralling downwards as she pulled the plug, thinking of Wakewater's many curiosities. After the ambulance had taken Manon away, she'd hardly given any thought to the leak that had driven her up to Manon's flat in the first place. She'd been preoccupied fussing over Sahara. When she remembered and had gone to confront the damage, she saw that the water had miraculously stopped again. Climbing onto the bed, she'd run her hands over the seemingly dry ceiling. There was not the tiniest trace of water.

And wasn't it odd that Manon had fallen in the first place? It wasn't as if she was a delicate old lady; she was dextrous enough not to unsettle her maze of books and paperwork. And she always seemed to take such precautions regarding water: leaving her outdoor clothes and shoes outside her front door, her raincoats and umbrellas – anything that had so much as touched the river. Then there was the fact that she'd so recently acquired a cat, with their innate fear of water. And the sticks she habitually picked from the riverbank, as if arming herself before she wound her way down towards the water. Ready for battle.

What was it that she had said – *push them down.*

Who was it that needed to be pushed down? Who was Manon afraid off? Kirsten thought of the figure beside the river and watched as the water in the tub drained away. She didn't need to go back to the window to see if the woman was there because she knew that for now, she was below the water.

14

Evelyn

THERE WAS A knock at the door. Evelyn sank deeper into the bed sheets. It was surely too early to begin her treatment. The room was pitch black. Mary must have made a mistake, she'd have to take her wet sheets elsewhere. The knocking persisted and Evelyn found herself sitting upright. Why couldn't she be left alone? She understood how Melusine felt. All she wanted was to sink away from the world, to lie back and uncoil her monstrous tail. But the world wouldn't let her be, there was always someone trying to get in.

'Evelyn,' she heard outside the door.

It wasn't Mary's voice. Evelyn thought of the woman she'd seen in the cooling room and beside the river, with her wet dark hair. Was she at her door now, begging to be let in?

'Evelyn,' the voice repeated, 'it's Blanche.'

Evelyn stumbled from her bed and made her way across the room. As she opened the door she saw Blanche illuminated by the candle she held in her palm, dressed similarly to Evelyn in a white nightgown.

'What are you doing here?'

'I couldn't sleep,' Blanche replied, making her way into the room and closing the door. She set the candle down on the bedside table and climbed into Evelyn's bed. 'It's cold,' she said, snuggling into the warm sheets.

Evelyn stared at her.

'Well, get in,' Blanche said. 'I won't stay long.'

Evelyn hesitated. What if someone had seen Blanche sneak into her room? What was she thinking, placing them both at the risk of impropriety? Then Evelyn remembered what Blanche had told her about her lost daughter. Perhaps the child's cries were keeping her awake.

She got into bed beside her. In the candlelight she could see Blanche smiling, though her eyes seemed solemn.

'I'm not frightened,' she began, 'it's just I've been thinking about a few things.'

'Oh?'

'I told you about Mrs Wilmot complaining about the bath-water?'

Evelyn nodded; there had been some problem with the piping, Dr Porter had told them; the water that filled her bath had been brown and slimy, as if the Thames had gushed from Wakewater's taps unrefined.

'Yesterday I saw Mrs Wilmot in the solarium. What I didn't realise was that she had got into the bath, filthy as it was. She swears that the water was crystal clear when she stepped into it.'

Evelyn pulled the sheets about her more tightly.

'Dr Porter said that she must have been seeing things and he gave her a sedative.' Mrs Wilmot didn't seem to be the imaginative type. It was unlikely she would have made something like that up.

'And then I remembered what Mrs Everett told me when I first arrived,' she continued. 'That sometimes when she was laying in warm bath water, all of the sudden the water would turn shockingly cold, as if a great deal of ice had just been heaped into the tub. She would jump out of it for fear of catching her death.'

Evelyn watched Blanche's expression carefully. There was excitement there, mingled with the fear.

'I thought she was an eccentric sort and I didn't think anything of it, until today.' Blanche paused for a moment. Evelyn touched her arm gently.

'Go on?'

'I saw Mrs Goddard at breakfast and she was telling the most curious story. Dr Porter had prescribed her a blanket packing and she let Mary wrap her up in thick sheets from head to toe, before Mary placed the spirit lamp underneath her chair. She perspired a great deal and felt good for it, her negative fluids all purged away. While this was going on, she chatted to Mary, who was sitting on the other side of the room. But when the heat became too unbearable and she pulled the sheet down from her face, you won't believe, there was no one in the room. When Mary returned, she said that she had left almost as soon as Mrs Goddard was settled, on some errand or other.'

Evelyn shivered but not from the cold. Blanche moved closer in the bed, bringing her warmth with her.

'So who had she been talking to?'

Evelyn didn't know what to say. She thought of the figure with the wet hair. Even though she hadn't seen her since the cooling room incident, she was never far from her thoughts. Sometimes she fancied that if she stared at the water long enough, the woman would materialise before her. Sometimes she wondered if she was following her around, just out of sight, concealed in the shadows, leaving wet footprints in her wake.

She was sick of shadows. Here was Blanche in her bed, as real as could be. Wide-eyed and trembling. She remembered kissing her beneath the apple trees.

'I saw someone I couldn't possibly have seen,' Evelyn began, 'down by the river and in the cooling room.'

'Someone you lost?'

'Yes.'

'What was her name?' Evelyn looked at Blanche with surprise. Was it that apparent that she could only love women?

'Milly. But I called her Melusine.'

'Melusine,' Blanche repeated. 'How did she die?'

'She jumped in the river and drowned.'

15

Kirsten

KIRSTEN WALKED BESIDE the river. She was determined not to let the last few days spoil Wakewater for her. She tried not to think too much about what Manon had said before she'd been taken away in the ambulance. She wanted to enjoy the river for what it was. She walked past the spot where she had glimpsed the strange woman the night before. She considered picking up a large stick as Manon had advised. Perhaps she needed it. *Push them down. Push them back down.*

Kirsten dismissed it from her mind. There was no one about. It was just her and the river. It was still very cold, the sky like dull steel. Occasionally the sun burst through the grey haze and brightened the river. Then Kirsten could see the troughs and peaks, the shimmer across the surface. Though she didn't really want to, she cut away from the path and made her way down the bank. She needed to look into the water, to convince herself that there was nothing to fear in its depths.

The ground was muddier than before and she edged her way carefully through the bramble bushes and low bracken to the waterfront. She squatted down, watching as the water lapped against the bank. Was it stirred up, as Manon had said, full of oestrogen, feminising the water? Kirsten had read about the increase in oestrogen levels in the water supply, caused by the extra hormones women excrete in their urine when on the contraceptive pill. She placed her hand in the water and waved it back and forth. If this was the case, was it a permissible consequence for women gaining control of their fertility? That the water should pay?

Kirsten had spent her entire adult life on one variety of contraceptive pill or another. There was something freeing and at the same time constraining about dispensing with the responsibility of thinking about having children. Kirsten wouldn't have had it any other way; she was grateful to live in a time when women had such choices. But becoming pregnant wasn't down to nature's plan alone anymore; it was dependent on human will and the cessation of hormones the female body had come to expect. Sometimes she wondered how many children she and Lewis would have conceived in their ten-year relationship if it wasn't for that little sugar-coated pill. Had they been meant to make a child together?

She'd missed a pill here and there over the years. When they started to have problems she'd become quite slack in taking it, blaming it on stress. She hadn't worried about it especially, assuming that their relationship was secure enough to deal with any eventuality. Perhaps part of her had wanted to become pregnant, but she was too afraid to take that next step, to make the decision to wean herself off birth control entirely. These accidents were as close as it could get to ever being natural. But it wasn't meant to be and Kirsten, watching the water now, was painfully aware of her age, of her chances of conceiving should she meet someone new. She wondered if she had let her only shot at motherhood slip away.

She moved away from the water and towards the west wing. But she wasn't ready to go back inside. She made her way through the gate Manon had shown her, into the courtyard and across the front of the house into Wakewater's vast grounds. She was the sole resident and part of her wanted to walk away from it all, from the house and the river, towards the trees and the distant hills.

She hadn't ventured far from the house, and doing so now she saw what an immense section of land Wakewater commanded. But no matter how far inland she seemed to go, the rise of the land meant that the river was nearly always within view. She could appreciate now how pivotal it was to Wakewater's existence, how close the building had been built to the river. Hadn't those Victorian architects worried about subsidence or flooding? Compared with the other buildings on the waterfront, which Kirsten could see in the distance, Wakewater was strikingly near to the water, as if it were taunting the river, defying its authority.

Kirsten wound her way back towards the house, making her way through what appeared to be an orchard. The boughs were empty, skeletal. She weaved her way through, the outstretched branches attempting to entangle her. And then as the path cleared, Kirsten saw the woman with the dark hair.

She was standing by the riverside, staring in Kirsten's direction. Kirsten could see her more clearly than before. She appeared to be wearing a long green dress. It looked old-fashioned and was torn and frayed. Her hair hung loose about her shoulders, slick and glossy as if it was wet. In fact, despite the distance, Kirsten was convinced that it was wet, dripping down onto her dress.

Kirsten only paused for a moment, changing direction from her intended course towards the river to take a more direct route back to the west wing. She walked fast but with control, all the while trying to rationalise what she had seen. There was no reason to be afraid of a woman with wet hair. It was perfectly normal for someone to walk along that public path by the river, even a curious kind of woman, dressed in such an odd way.

Without breaking her stride she cast a glance over her shoulder towards the spot beside the river.

The woman was gone.

Kirsten stopped and looked around. Where had she disappeared to? Perhaps back the way she had come along the bridleway. Just then it began to rain and Kirsten saw her.

She was in the orchard, where Kirsten had just been. She could never have covered that much ground while Kirsten's back was turned. And she was closer now than before, in the grounds of Wakewater.

Kirsten picked up her pace, trying her best not to break into a run. She began to dig in her pockets for her keys; she wanted to be inside and to close the door against this strange figure and the panic that was mounting inside of her. As she approached the west wing, with *Wakewater Apartments* emblazoned in blue lettering, she fought the desire to look behind her. She struggled with the keys, her fingers cold from the rain.

It was then that she noticed. Through the glass door she could see the lobby illuminated. The entrance lighting was activated through movement, but there couldn't be anyone inside.

Kirsten was the only resident.

The light went off and then flickered on again, breaking into an incessant blinking. It must be some kind of loose wire, she reasoned, as the key finally slid into the keyhole.

But she had paused long enough outside the entrance to feel that the strange woman had narrowed the distance between them. As clearly as she could feel the rain trickling against her skin, she could sense someone at her back.

She turned slowly.

There was no one there.

It was with relief that she opened the door, swinging it wide and stepping out of the rain. But in the blinking light, she could see that the floor tiles were covered in a film of water. It had been dry when she left. There was no one else here to leave any marks. But there, across the lobby floor, was a trail of wet footprints.

16

Evelyn

'MELUSINE. MELUSINE,' EVELYN whispered into Milly's ear. They lay entwined in bed, their clothes cast over a chair. Evelyn had acquired some temporary lodgings for Milly: a set of rooms in a modest part of town, away from the disreputable haunts that Milly was more used to. Milly couldn't have stayed in the refuge indefinitely, and until Evelyn managed to secure her some work in service, this seemed like the most suitable answer. She had never imagined that she'd be spending so much time in these rooms as well.

Milly smiled and sank deeper into Evelyn's embrace. She let Evelyn stroke her long dark hair, brushing the tendrils from her face. It was the middle of the afternoon. They'd pulled the flimsy curtains against the sunlight, but it still filtered through. It felt so blissfully wicked, lying in bed in the middle of the day. Love didn't adhere to clock time. These few hours each day had become such a welcome delight to Evelyn. When she was at the refuge or back in her father's house, she knew that Milly was here, safely ensconced in these little rooms, waiting for her to return. It was such a singular feeling, knowing that somebody was missing you, counting the hours until you came back to them.

Evelyn stretched, 'I've got to go soon.'

'No, no,' Milly replied, sleepily. That was the only drawback. She was becoming more despondent each time Evelyn had to leave. Evelyn could understand why. Though Milly had made it clear how thankful she was to have left that life behind, how indebted she was, she relied entirely now on Evelyn for her happiness. She didn't know anyone in the neighbourhood and the old friends she'd kept would not have been welcome in this part of town. She wasn't used to her own time. She had no education; no way to channel her introspection

'I've got to attend a Rescue Society meeting,' Evelyn said, sitting upright.

'There's no need, you've already rescued someone.'

Evelyn smiled and kissed her lightly. 'There are more souls to be saved.' She climbed out of bed, slipping her dress over her smock. Milly grabbed her by the hand.

'Don't worry about those other girls, just save me.'

Evelyn laughed, 'But you are saved, my Melusine.'

Milly frowned and sank back into the bed. Sometimes she acted like such a child.

Evelyn sat beside her. 'I'll never let you go back to that life, I promise.'

'Then take me with you?'

Evelyn hesitated; part of her wanted to. The Rescue Society opened its arms to fallen women; she'd be welcome there. But another part of her wondered if her feelings would be too transparent and everyone would know what existed between them. She couldn't risk that. She desperately wanted to keep this bit of herself secret and locked away from the rest of the world. She shook her head.

'I don't mind you parading me around,' Milly continued, 'as an example of one of your reformed girls.'

Evelyn smiled. 'I don't think it's a good idea.'

Now Milly got out of bed. She strode across the room on lithe limbs, snatching at her clothes. There was a confidence in her nakedness, as if she knew the power she exerted on those who gazed upon her. Evelyn was struck again at how perfect and unblemished her body was, despite the many ways it had been mistreated.

'And what am I supposed to do while you save all the whores in London?' she asked.

'Milly, please...'

'I'm nothing but a kept woman.' She stepped into her dress, fastening it with speed, as perhaps she'd had to do once too often.

Evelyn laughed. 'I am not one of your gentlemen callers who pays for your services.'

'But you do pay. You pay for me to stay here, in this prison. You pay to keep me all to yourself.'

Evelyn sat down on the bed, stung. Was that how Milly saw their relationship, as some kind of exchange? She was so used to selling her body that perhaps she had no idea that love was given for free. For the briefest of moments, Evelyn wondered if Milly had been performing a part, acting the role of a lover in exchange for bed and board.

'Milly, I do it for you, not for myself.'

But Milly was already striding toward the stairs, struggling with the ribbons of her bonnet.

'Where will you go?' Evelyn called. The door slammed in reply.

17

Kirsten

KIRSTEN OPENED MANON'S door. She'd arranged for a locksmith and Manon had given her a set of keys when she'd visited her in hospital. The fall had done more damage than it was first assumed, but Manon was healing well. She hoped to be home soon. Until then there was a wealth of knowledge about Wakewater and its secrets just within Kirsten's reach. She knew Manon would understand. Stepping over the piles of books that littered the threshold, Kirsten made her way inside.

It made sense to begin in the study, though there was so much information scattered throughout the flat that could also prove useful. She wasn't quite sure what she was looking for, but she guessed that if she was going to understand more about the river, the study was probably the best place to start. The flat was still unnaturally warm, despite the heating being turned off. The study especially seemed to radiate heat; the papers and books incubating the secret knowledge Kirsten hoped to garner. She started at the desk. A series of Post-it notes had been stuck against the veneer. She glanced over them, deciphering Manon's frantic handwriting:

> *- Birth and Water - In Summerian, the word for 'sea' is the same as the word for 'womb', both 'mar'.*
> *- The Maya and Ancient Egyptians thought that their worlds originated with the waters of the primordium.*

Kirsten looked towards a pile of binders instead. She lifted one folder and a dozen postcards and pictures slipped through their plastic envelope and onto the floor. She crouched to pick them up.

Mostly reprints of Victorian paintings, they displayed an array of women in water. There were some images she recognised, like Waterhouse's *Lady of Shalott* depicting the eponymous heroine's last voyage upon the water, and others that Kirsten had never seen before. What was striking about them however was that they all portrayed women as being frail and weak. Looking through the scattered images, she recognised the sickly pallor of the consumptive; the anorexic archetype that had become so fashionable. They seemed to promoting the idea that the most beautiful woman was a dead one. She rummaged through the pile and drew out Millais' *Ophelia.* Now this was a painting she was familiar with. How often had she spent her lunch break at the Tate, staring across at Millais' most famous work, watching the crowds of school children and tourists gaze at Ophelia's floating corpse, the bridal wreath she'd made drifting alongside her.

She'd read how Millais' model, Lizzie Siddal, had lain in a bathtub to provide a more realistic impression for the artist.

Kirsten wondered what Lizzie had thought about lying for hours in that cold water, pretending to be a dead girl. Perhaps her thoughts had turned from Ophelia to all the other spurned women who ended up in the river. Could she hear them calling to her beneath the surface, pulling her down to join them? Lizzie had contracted pneumonia after sitting for Millais and overdosed a few years later on opium. Perhaps she'd never been able to escape the weight of the water after that, of the slippery feeling of death.

Kirsten sighed. It was like wading through Manon's mind. But where were the viragos, the temptresses, the sirens and nymphs? Manon didn't have any of images of those women, though Kirsten knew that the mythical ones resided in the water too.

Returning *Ophelia* to the pile, Kirsten brushed against a leather-bound notebook. She opened it, knowing at once it was what she was looking for. It was filled with Manon's scribbled notes, a little unorganised, though it seemed to include a list of various mythical water women. Under the heading 'Rusalki' Manon had written:

> *Rusalki are Slavic water spirits. It is believed that when women die in or close to water, especially those who have committed suicide or those who have been intentionally drowned by others, they often return to haunt that particular body of water. Women who are pregnant at the time of their death are believed to be especially potent. Typical of water women, they lure mortals with their song, usually entangling them in their long hair. They rarely leave the water but have been known to dwell amongst the trees,*

sometimes climbing them. Rusalki are known for their long wet hair, which lends them an immortality away from the water. If their hair dries, they expire.

Kirsten closed the book and smiled.

18

Evelyn

EVELYN PLACED HER hand over her mouth to stifle the laughter. Blanche had buried her head into Evelyn's shoulder, but it did little to stem the sound of her giggling. They were standing at Evelyn's bedroom door, Blanche still in her nightgown, trying to stage her escape. The house was already awake and they could hear the other guests making their way down to breakfast. Evelyn was fully dressed - though it had taken much longer than normal due to Blanche's caresses - ready to check that the coast was clear or to provide a distraction while Blanche snuck out. It had been reckless allowing her to stay the night. Now they had to run the gauntlet to get her back to her room.

It wasn't a laughing matter, but they had woken up so light-hearted and carefree. Embarrassed that they had shared so much the night before, self-conscious that they had woken to find their bodies intertwined, Evelyn hardly cared what happened now. She felt so deliriously happy that Blanche was here; what was impropriety compared to this feeling?

It was a feeling she knew. She'd felt it before but had lost it. That had been her mistake; she'd locked her love in a room, hoping that was enough to keep it safe. But she'd stifled it instead and it had flown. She hadn't expected to feel this way again and she knew now that love needed a little space. She was prepared to let Blanche go.

'Let's try again,' Evelyn said, her hand on the door handle.

Blanche nodded in reply, before giggling once more. Laughing seemed to be the only thing to counter the fear of being caught.

'I'm going to go out and see if anyone's around,' Evelyn said, holding her by the waist, 'then I'll signal to you to follow.'

Blanche smiled, breathing deeply. 'Yes. I'm ready.'

Evelyn opened the door as soundlessly as possible and slipped out onto the landing. She heard Mrs Goddard's approach before she saw her and closed the door swiftly behind her.

'Good morning, Mrs Goddard,' she said, slightly louder than normal, hoping Blanche would hear.

'Good morning, my dear. Are you heading down to breakfast?'

Evelyn wavered, struggling for an excuse. Her back against the door as if guarding it. 'Yes,' she said finally, falling into step. It seemed better to divert Mrs Goddard and provide Blanche with the opportunity to make her getaway.

In the dining room, Mrs Miller served a simple fare of porridge and toast. In keeping with Wakewater's philosophy, breakfast was a relaxed affair and punctuality wasn't strictly observed. Only a handful of guests were gathered around the table.

'I must say, the water is doing wonders,' Mrs Goddard announced cheerfully, 'but I can't wait to have sausage and bacon again.'

Mrs Wilmot concurred and Evelyn watched as other women

fell into conversation. She wasn't interested in small talk; her mind drifted back up the stairs to Blanche and her memories of the night before.

'Mrs Arden's late this morning,' Mrs Wilmot said quietly at Evelyn's side. It was true; Blanche was usually one of the first to breakfast; she didn't like to miss out on any potential gossip. Evelyn shrugged, feeling her blood rush to her cheeks. Everyone knew that she and Blanche were friends; there was nothing implied in the remark, she told herself. But Blanche wasn't the only one with an appetite for gossip. She wondered if anyone had seen them in the orchard, or had heard them giggling in her bedroom.

At that point Blanche walked in, looking fresh and radiant, not at all capable of clandestine visits in the night. She shot Evelyn a playful glance as she sat down.

Dr Porter often breakfasted earlier than everyone else; his plate was empty save for a few crumbs, and a newspaper lay in his stead. Mrs Miller had set about gathering the crockery and reached for the paper.

'Now, now, let's have a look at what's going on in the outside world,' Mrs Goddard said, taking it off of her. Mrs Wilmot tutted. Though not forbidden, most of Wakewater's guests had been prescribed a course of ignorance – no intellectual stimulation allowed under any circumstances, which especially included reading. At Wakewater, the rest of the world didn't exist. The river truly was a moat, protecting its charges from the dangers of outside.

'Another poor wretch pulled from the river,' Mrs Goddard sighed, stretching out the broadsheet.

'You should ask Evelyn,' Blanche said, helping herself to a

slice of toast. 'She's done a lot of work with the Rescue Society, trying to save *those* kinds of women.' The comment was well intended and Blanche smiled as she said it. But seeing the look on Evelyn's face, she realised how tactless her remark had been, especially considering what Evelyn had disclosed the night before.

'It's ... very charitable,' she stammered.

'I hardly think this is a suitable topic to discuss in company,' Mrs Wilmot said. Evelyn sat upright. She was used to this argument. How often had respectable women refused to listen to what was really going on, hiding behind the pretext of decorum and etiquette.

Mrs Goddard laughed. 'It's only us women. If we can't talk about these things amongst ourselves, the men have truly won.'

'But it's hardly ladylike,' Mrs Wilmot retorted.

Nor was the notion of selling you body, Evelyn thought, but the women she met didn't have that choice. They had not been born with a lady's privileges, to fret over propriety and respectability.

Mrs Wilmot lifted a serviette to the corner of her mouth. 'I admire your efforts,' she said, directing her attention to Evelyn, 'but I fear there is not enough water in the world to cleanse those poor girls.'

'The water is where most of them will end up, sadly.' Evelyn stood. 'Excuse me.'

She made her way back up the stairs to her room, hardly caring that she'd left the table in such an obviously irate manner. That morning she'd woken up in Blanche's arms feeling so untroubled, but now she could feel only anger swelling inside her. Just when she'd begun to forget Milly, Blanche had dragged her back out of the water.

For the first time since being at Wakewater, Evelyn craved the river. She wanted to walk alongside it, to lose her thoughts in its gentle undulations, to get away from the house and all of its guests, Blanche included.

She opened the door but hesitated on the threshold. Across the room, the bathtub was full to the brim with water – though Mary had not been instructed to draw one – and the water was an unnatural sickly green. As she made her way closer, she saw that it was actually her green dress, spread heavily across the surface. Evelyn made her way closer, recoiling as she touched the fabric; the material was wet and slimy. She reached in again and hauled the dress out. It was much heavier than normal because of the water, which poured off of the fabric in vast quantities, draining back into the now half-full tub. But Evelyn could see that the water that remained was the murky colour of the river.

Evelyn sighed. Her green dress was ruined. The fabric completely saturated, the dress itself torn and frayed, ripped in parts as if it had been caught on rocks and other obstacles, dragged along the riverbed. In fact, the dress had taken on the sheen of the river; it looked as if had spent an age beneath the water, not a few moments in bathwater.

Evelyn heard a knock at the door and turned to see Blanche on the threshold.

'I'm so sorry,' she began, 'I wasn't thinking...'

Evelyn looked back at the green dress in her arms.

'Get out!' she screamed. 'Get out!'

19

Kirsten

KIRSTEN LAY IN bed, Manon's notebook across her lap. She hadn't ventured out for a couple of days, hibernating inside with only Manon's research and Sahara for company. The heating was on full power and she kicked the covers off her legs. But it was better to be too hot. She didn't want to encourage the water in.

She turned a page and one of Manon's copious Post-it notes fell against the sheets. She picked it up before Sahara tried to lick it.

A Water Doctor is a physiological practitioner, it read, and underneath she'd written *Water Doctor – Quack Doctor. Quack, quack, quack*, and had drawn some ducks along the bottom. Maybe Manon's mind wasn't as sound as she thought.

She placed the Post-it back inside and resumed flicking through the pages. On one was stuck a photocopy of a poem entitled 'The Bridge of Sighs'. In the margin she recognised Manon's scribbled hand:

Thomas Hood's sentimental treatment of the 'fallen woman' theme.

Kirsten skimmed the poem as Sahara jumped up onto the bed and curled onto her lap.

The bleak wind of March
Made her tremble and shiver;
But not the dark arch,
Or the black flowing river:
Mad from life's history
Glad to death's mystery,
Swift to be hurl'd –
Anywhere, anywhere
Out of the world!

She couldn't read anymore. It was a rather morbid subject, though she expected nothing less from Manon. Beneath it was an image, a glossy reprint that had been torn from a book. It portrayed a young woman lying half in the water, half against the ground, as if she had just been washed up by the river. She was framed by the arch of a bridge and her arms were outstretched, with the hand closest to the viewer clutched around something. Perhaps a keepsake of some kind. Was it a necklace or a locket? Beneath the painting, Manon had written in her spidery scrawl, *George Frederic Watts 'Found Drowned'*.

Kirsten got out of bed, and Sahara followed, weaving in and out of her feet as she made her way to the window. Kirsten had had enough of the water, its presence taunted her, making her aware of this sudden entrapment. She supposed she could go down to the river, but she knew what she would see there. The woman with the long wet hair. Was she really a water spirit, a rusalka? It seemed better not to find out.

She shut the curtains in the front room and made her way

into the spare room to do the same. But she paused as she crossed the threshold, realising that her feet were wet. Despite the heat of the flat, she hadn't been able to keep the water out. A film of water had spread across the floor. Luckily there wasn't much that could be damaged, only the legs of furniture and the last removal box that she hadn't got round to unpacking. Because she didn't want to unpack it.

In it was heaped all the mementoes and reminders of her relationship with Lewis. All the things she'd discovered squirreled away in various other innocuous looking boxes. But she'd collated them all now, all in one place for her to deal with, when the time was right.

The water seemed to have got to it first.

From across the hallway she heard Sahara hiss. She saw her pad towards the threshold but back away again at the sight of the water.

'It's alright, girl,' Kirsten said. But it wasn't. She crouched to inspect the damage. The cardboard was soaked through, the box full to the brim with water.

'Shit, shit,' she said, and she heard Sahara mew in reply. She rolled up her sleeve and cast her hand into the box, water gushing up over the rim. Her fingers found a photo frame and, pulling it out, she saw that the photograph was ruined. Lewis' face had been partially washed away. She fished around some more, retrieving objects that were irrevocably watermarked, lining them up on the floor like a beachcomber's treasure. It felt like a strange lucky dip, seeing which items had acquired the least damage. Eventually her fingers clasped the cold metal of the locket Lewis had given her and, salvaging it from the water, she saw once again the inscription that was there; the pledge of everlasting love. She wanted to drop it back into the box but instead she opened the clasp. There was nothing inside anymore, except for the water.

20

Evelyn

EVELYN HAD HUNG the green dress up on a peg on the back of the door. Despite the late summer heat, it didn't seem to be drying out. In fact, if anything it was as wet as when she had pulled it from the bath. She watched the dress now by candlelight as she lay in bed, puddles converging beneath it.

She didn't try to rationalise it. The dress was just another part of Wakewater's strangeness, its ability to tap into the anxieties of its residents. The dress belonged with her memories of Milly, and she found herself recalling that night in Milly's lodgings when she'd let her try it on. It was the first time they'd undressed in front of one another and she could still bring to mind that panicked delight as she watched Milly remove the layers, her hidden self suddenly revealed.

Except that Evelyn hadn't seen all of her. Not really. She hadn't seen what was really hidden beneath the crinoline and whalebones, beneath her soft white flesh. She only saw that when Milly was pulled dead from the river; then there was no denying it: her stomach swollen not just with the river water but because of the child she carried.

But Wakewater had revived her. It had brought Milly

back. If Milly could step out of the river, it was not implausible that Evelyn's green dress could find itself immersed in that same element. In a way, the dress should have belonged to Milly; she had loved its emerald allure more than Evelyn ever had. It seemed strangely fitting that she would reclaim it now, that the dress should share the same fate as its rightful owner, dragged through the river to be washed up, faded and ruined.

Evelyn rolled over in bed, away from the dress. Perhaps this was what she deserved, this life at Wakewater: a watery purgatory, drenched, soaked, saturated in the same element that had taken her love. How often had she'd lain in one of the many baths she'd been prescribed as part of her Water Cure and considered sinking down beneath the surface. Of lying there, beneath it all, watching the bubbles floating to the surface eventually cease. What kept her from letting go?

Blanche.

Evelyn sighed. They hadn't spoken since the morning when Evelyn had shouted at her. The memory of it gave Evelyn a sinking feeling inside. Blanche hadn't really done anything wrong; Evelyn should have welcomed any platform to talk about her work with the Rescue Society. But it felt too raw after what they had shared the night before, and then seeing the ruined dress, it was as if Milly was telling her something. Milly had always been a jealous kind of woman.

But Milly was dead. Blanche was here in the present, warm and open, and capable of loving her back. Evelyn sat up, wondering if she'd ruined yet another chance of happiness. Perhaps it wasn't too late for her to remedy.

She pulled herself out of bed and reached for the candle on

the nightstand. Casting a shawl over her nightdress, she made her way to the door, sliding past the drenched green dress. The water that pooled from it had formed a line across the threshold.

Evelyn stepped over it and into the hallway. The candlelight illuminated the otherwise pitch-black corridor and she made her way slowly, cautious of the shadows that gathered in the recesses.

She hesitated outside Blanche's room and then knocked.

There was no sound inside, so Evelyn knocked again, slightly harder. She pushed the door lightly, expecting it to be locked, but it gave way. She recalled the previous night when Blanche had snuck into her room and thought how odd it was that she was doing the same. She hoped she wouldn't mind the intrusion. Holding the candle tentatively against the dark, she stepped inside.

Blanche wasn't alone.

In the candlelight, Evelyn could make out a figure hunched over Blanche, her legs crouched over her waist, her wet hair dripping down onto her face. Her hands were clutched around Blanche's throat, squeezing tighter. At Evelyn's approach, the figure turned, her black hair clipping through the air, and with a wild look in her eyes, she hissed at Evelyn.

'Milly, no, no!' Evelyn ran towards the bed.

The woman relinquished her grip on Blanche in an instant and recoiled in one fluid movement, like a wave receding from the shore. Evelyn ran to Blanche's side, running her hands over her shoulders, her neck, shaking her gently awake.

'Blanche! Blanche!'

She lay immobile, frozen. Slowly, she opened her eyes, and as she registered Evelyn's face, her eyes filled with panic.

She reached for her throat and sat up in bed struggling for breath. Evelyn stroked her back and looked about the room for Melusine. Only shadows gazed back.

21

Kirsten

KIRSTEN NUDGED THE door to the old part of the house with her hip as Manon had shown her. It opened wide enough for her to slide through. She made her way inside, into what had once been a kitchen. She groped in her cardigan pocket for the torch she'd taken from Manon's, but instead her hand brushed something metallic and cold: the locket she'd picked up that she intended to throw out with the rubbish. She fished inside the other pocket. Retrieving the torch, she shone it into the darkness and Wakewater was suddenly illuminated.

She made her way through the house as cautiously as before. The building was too dilapidated, too rundown for Kirsten to feel safe. It didn't help that she was haunted by the water and by the creature she believed inhabited it. There was nothing safe about Wakewater. But if she was going to understand it, she needed to know more about its past.

She followed the pipes. She couldn't understand the strange, watery phenomena in her flat, the fact the water always found a way in, despite her best efforts, so seeing where the pipes led to, she decided, may help make sense of things. She followed their network down through the west wing and realised that they would converge under the main building. It seemed likely that the Turkish bath, with its elaborate fountain, would have been built with close access to this underground system.

The room itself wasn't far from the side entrance, but Kirsten realised that she had explored very little of Wakewater House. She found herself walking in the opposite direction instead, toward a set of stairs. As she ascended, daylight flooded the corridor, entering the building from a series of overly large windows at the end of the hallway.

It was a grand room, comprised almost entirely of glass. Some of the windows had sustained damage over the years, but they didn't detract at all from the main draw: the exceptional view. From this height you could see the river stretching back for miles and miles. Kirsten made her way towards one of the windows, leaning against the pane and looking down into the dark, winding current. But it didn't feel close enough. There was a door to a balcony. She pulled against the rusted bolt and pushed the door wide.

The cold air greeted her. The balcony was large, running the entire length of the glass room, easily able to accommodate numerous patio chairs and tables in the summertime. She imagined that Wakewater's guests would have spent a great deal of time out here. Kirsten edged out towards the railing, unable to resist the urge to look over the edge. The air seemed to rush up past her, blowing her back towards the house. The river looked wilder from this height, the current churning and swirling. She gripped the railing tighter and stared into the torrent; there was something mesmerising about gazing out over the precipice. She almost forgot her fear of the water.

A sound like a wail gave from the metal and Kirsten felt

herself lurch forward. The railing drooped towards the water and Kirsten flung herself back on to the balcony floor. The metal sighed again, this time with the sound of splintering wood. She got to her feet cautiously, aware now that the platform she stood on was far from stable. Making her way back slowly to the door, she cursed herself for taking such a risk when she knew what a sorry state the house was in. She could easily have fallen.

She felt relieved once she was back inside the glass room. She didn't look at the river as she closed the door, though she could see its dark impression refracted in the glass panels, in the glittering beads of the chandeliers she passed beneath. The water had permeated every corner of Wakewater, and though she wanted to turn her back on the river and its strange influence on her life, Wakewater forced her to look on. Even when she closed her eyes it was there, slick and ominous, floating through her mind.

She retraced her steps along the corridor and made her way back to the room with the fountain. It was just as she remembered it: the grand centrepiece, the elaborate tiling and wainscoting. This time she looked more closely at the wall tiles; a green and blue design that resembled the swirling movement of the waves, and she could see what remained of a mosaic on the far wall. Through the disrepair, she could make out a large, scaly fish tail.

She walked through the water that puddled in the middle of the room. Kirsten was used to having wet feet by now. She ran her finger between the peaks of the waves carved along the edge of the fountain. The water inside the basin was dark and stagnant, eerily still as if it had been untroubled for many years.

Looking into the pool was like looking into the dark interior of a well. There was a sense of curious endlessness. How deep did it go?

Despite the grimy appearance, Kirsten wanted to touch the water. She let her hand sink deeper, sweeping the muck and detritus from the surface, needing clarity, almost willing the water to reveal its intentions.

The fountain burst to life. Water shot violently from the uppermost spout, surging upwards before raining down heavily on Kirsten, who edged backwards to avoid the deluge. But she was soaked through in seconds, her heart racing with the cold shock of the water. She tried to peer through the cascade to the water bubbling in the basin. But the surface was even more obscured than before, agitated into peaks and troughs like the intricate waves carved into the marble.

Kirsten felt the water at her feet vibrate, bubbling along the surface of the floor tiles with no hope of escape. The drains must be blocked. She would have to go deeper.

There had to be access to a basement. She made her way, wet as she was, through Wakewater's passages, following doors that led to more cavernous rooms and back again to the main hallway. She was beginning to feel like Wakewater was turning her around and around, as if she were caught in the inescapable current of the river. She tried one last doorway and smiled when she saw a staircase leading downwards.

She was descending into the depths of the house now and there was something frightening about falling further from the daylight. A strange feeling overcame her, that she'd be sealed beneath the surface, immersed inside the house. She fought the feeling away as she wound her way deeper. She had to see where the pipes led. She had to know what was at the heart of Wakewater.

At the bottom was a modestly sized room, unexceptional architecturally compared to the other rooms Kirsten had seen, but it contained the most curious object positioned in the centre.

It looked to be some kind of swimming pool, made of metal with raised sides, like an oversized bath that would allow you to stretch out and swim a little if you chose. But it didn't convey a sense of leisure; the cold metal surface made it look like something distinctly medical. She ran her hand over the hard surface, her fingertips catching against a series of sharp edges.

Crouching down, she shone the torch against the tank. There was something inscribed in the metal. It looked like the marks had been made by something sharp, like a knife. Just one word.

Melusine.

22

Evelyn

EVELYN WAITED IN the orchard. Blanche had eluded her for the last few days and there was no certainty she would come now. Evelyn had tried to explain her presence in Blanche's room when she'd seen Milly hunched over Blanche like some kind of succubus. She could still recall her wet hair dripping down onto Blanche's face, her fingers coiled around her throat.

Blanche had listened, but Evelyn could tell she didn't believe her. She'd taken to wearing more formal high-necked blouses, not at all in keeping with the way she usually dressed, but at least they covered the bruises around her throat. It made her look more reserved, austere, not at all like the light-hearted young woman Evelyn had come to care for. But then, Blanche had seemed to acquire a guarded aspect to her countenance too. She was more cautious around Evelyn, as if she blamed her for the bruising. *You're not well,* she'd told her, raising her hand to her collar. *We should see less of each other, we need to concentrate on getting better.*

Evelyn sat down among the fallen apples. Perhaps Blanche did genuinely care for her. Otherwise she would have told Dr Porter what had happened and Evelyn would have been flung out of Wakewater for attacking a fellow patient, to be sent someplace much worse. For all that, it pained her that Blanche didn't believe her story.

She could understand why, she knew how far-fetched it sounded, talking about a woman coming out the water. But Evelyn had listened to all of Blanche's stories about the strange things that were happening at Wakewater, never doubting that she was haunted by the memory of her dead child. Perhaps, for all Blanche's talk, she was closed off to anything she couldn't readily comprehend.

Or perhaps she was frightened.

Evelyn stood. It was clear Blanche wasn't going to come today. She looked towards the river and there, beside the bank, stood Milly. Evelyn sighed. She didn't want to look at her but found that she couldn't quite turn away. Since the incident in Blanche's bedroom, Evelyn couldn't stop seeing Milly. She'd see her walking through the solarium, leaning against the balcony railing to look down into the water. She'd see her in the cooling room, sitting beside the fountain, or sometimes at her side as she bathed, running her pale, dead fingers through the water. And when she woke up, there she'd be, standing by the door, caressing the faded green gown. A gown as wet as she was. And she was always here, beside the river, waiting for Evelyn on the riverbank

Evelyn turned away from the water and made her way back to the house. Without Blanche's company, Wakewater felt like a prison. The only consolation was that at least there was a routine to adhere to. She was pulled through the day by nurses, sat in baths, wrapped in compresses, drenched and watered, chilled and steamed. It felt like she was biding her time, waiting to get back into Blanche's good graces. Waiting for the water to heal the rift between them.

As she approached the courtyard, she saw Blanche and Dr Porter come out of one of the side entrances. He held out his arm as they negotiated the stairs and Blanche laughed, accepting it. Evelyn was reminded of the first night she had met Blanche. How she had blushed in Dr Cardew's company, appearing to listen so attentively. She'd flung her head back then in the same coquettish manner. Dr Porter pointed towards the river with his cane, and they set off in its direction, walking side by side. Evelyn could hear Blanche's laughter echoing off the water.

She waited until they were some distance off before she made her way into the main building. She walked through Wakewater's labyrinthine corridors, past Mrs Miller clanging pots in the kitchen, winding her way deeper into the house. She fully expected Dr Porter's office to be locked, but he was a man who trusted his patients, confident in his power over them and over women in general. The gentler sex were too respectful, too timid to go sneaking amongst his things. But Evelyn had already transgressed, at least in the eyes of society. What was opening one more door?

It was a masculine space, designed to convey authority through the mahogany panelling and dark furniture. The walls were filled with books, books that none of Wakewater's female guests were ever permitted to read. She knew what she was looking for, though she didn't fully understand the strange impulse that had led her here.

She began to open Dr Porter's cabinets and drawers. Journals and medical textbooks seemed to pack every shelf and cavity. Her initial cautiousness was replaced by a sudden reckless desire to uncover his secrets. She knew they were in here, Blanche had told her so. Making her way systematically through the room, she hesitated upon opening yet another mahogany door. But there, displayed in a leather case, was what she had come to see.

The cabinet was full of obstetric and gynaecological instruments. They gleamed in the dark interior, like the river when sunlight skimmed its surface. There were a variety of scissors and callipers, forceps in various sizes, some hideously large. Scalpels lay encased in their leather holders alongside a series of sharp objects that resembled crochet hooks. Evelyn reached in towards what seemed to be the largest object in the collection, an eight-pronged cervical dilator. And beside it lay that other instrument of torture, the dreaded speculum.

She held the cold steel in her hand. She wondered if this instrument had seen as much action as the ones she knew were employed so regularly by the police and doctors in the lock hospitals on women suspected of prostitution to ascertain whether they had symptoms of venereal disease. Washed in a solution of potash and oiled before use, one speculum could be used on dozens of women in one day. Some who weren't prostitutes at all. Most women objected to the examination, though it went ahead regardless, often with force, whilst others were detained in prison until they consented.

Evelyn placed the speculum back down. Dr Porter's collection did seem more like something a torturer would prize than anything devised in the name of medicine. She imagined they hadn't seen much action since Dr Porter had become such a devoted practitioner of the Water Cure, and for that she was thankful.

It had been curiosity as much as anything that had driven Evelyn into Dr Porter's office, but now standing in front of this assemblage of steel, she knew she was meant to take something. Something he wouldn't miss. It seemed only fair since Dr Porter had stolen Blanche that she should take something back. She ran her fingers over the assortment of metal objects and pulled a scalpel from its leather sheath. Placing it in her pocket, she closed the door.

23

Kirsten

KIRSTEN DREAMT SHE was on the bank of a river. Beside her was a boat and along the prow was inscribed *Melusine*. Further along the bank stood the woman with the long dark hair, staring across the water. She was dressed in the green gown, but it didn't look wet or torn as it had done before. It almost seemed to sparkle in the twilight. She walked towards Kirsten and pointed to the other side of the river.

Kirsten didn't know what she expected her to do. The woman climbed aboard and sat down at the bow, waiting, staring out at the water once more. Kirsten saw the oars balanced against the sides and realised that she was meant to row her across. She clambered into the vessel and, using one of the oars, pushed them gently off.

The boat bobbed on the surface initially until Kirsten got her stride. Then it cut through the water with speed. Kirsten was glad that her strange companion had decided to face the water. There was something unnatural about her, about her ashen skin and her hair that seemed so dark it had to be wet. The woman pointed into the distance and that was the first time something hit the boat.

They both reeled from the impact. Careful not to drop the oars, Kirsten peered over the edge.

A figure lay face down in the water. It was a woman, entirely naked, her long hair billowing behind her in the current. She swayed with the movement of the water in time with the boat. Kirsten carefully extracted one of the oars, stood and tentatively prodded the body. It sank against the touch, the momentum propelling the body over so that it faced the surface.

Kirsten fell back into the boat.

The woman had been opened up. The incision began just under her breasts, and the skin had been pulled back to reveal a hollow space inside. Like the images of Anatomical Venuses Kirsten had seen in Manon's flat, all the neat parts inside had been taken out. The woman was completely hollow like the vessel Kirsten was sitting in. Kirsten stood on shaking legs and, looking around, saw that the river was littered with corpses. Hollow, floating women, bereft of what made them biologically female.

The woman with the long dark hair pointed into the distance once again, and Kirsten, numb with shock, resumed her position. She began to row once more, but their progress through the water was impeded by these floating, barren bodies. It was like cutting through a sea filled with ice floes. The corpses crashed against the prow and the small boat rocked wildly. Kirsten tried to avoid them, to push them aside with the oar, but there were too many. The strange women with the long dark hair continued to point into the distance and Kirsten knew that she had to keep going forwards, despite the dangers, despite her fears. Another collision set the boat rocking more violently than before and Kirsten felt a strange sense of the inevitable, that the boat would overturn and plunge her into the water.

24

Evelyn

EVELYN WOKE IN cold water. She'd been dreaming about the river and about Milly. In the dream Milly had been dressed in the gown of green taffeta, but it hadn't been ruined and torn as it was now. It looked as if it had just been made, the fabric shining with an emerald lustre. She looked like a mermaid, with the silk trail fanning out behind her. Milly had told Evelyn that she wanted to sail down the river, and there on the bank appeared a boat, the kind of flat-bottomed ones gentleman would punt along the Thames. Evelyn could not refuse her; she looked so enchanting in her green dress.

Evelyn assisted Milly into the boat and she stepped inside so lady-like, careful that the hem of her gown didn't touch the water. Evelyn picked up the oars and pushed them off, the action of rowing strangely familiar though she'd never done it before. She was vaguely aware as they inched their way deeper into the river that neither of them could swim. That if they fell overboard they would most certainly drown. But that had not been the worst of it. For in the water floated the most monstrous forms, hundreds of them, their bodies battering against the prow as it cut through the water. Using her oar, Evelyn had prodded one such figure bobbing along the surface, little more than debris on the current. It was a woman. But not a woman. Just the shell of a woman, really, hollowed out, devoid of her sex.

Evelyn sat up in the cold bath, shivering from the memory of the dream more than the temperature of the water. It had been warm before she fell asleep. She was alone in her bedroom, Mary had not returned from whatever errand had called her away. Evelyn reached into the water for the scalpel; it was still there, the metal even colder than the water.

Evelyn looked at her veins, blue like the river, and like the river her blood gushed along a network of tributaries. It would have been easier if the water was still warm. Mary had drawn such a hot bath that when she first stepped in the steam had obscured the green dress hanging by the door. It would have been easier in warm water for the blood to flow. She'd have hardly noticed it. She would have sank into the warmth and let her body drift downwards.

But the water was cold, like the river. And Evelyn had seen what floated along the river. It was better in the bath. In this little vessel, that would carry her toward death. She didn't want to be at Wakewater anymore, she just wanted to sink beneath the surface. She held the scalpel in front of her, examining the blade. It was designed for precision. Just one little cut.

Out of the corner of her eye, a shadow moved by the door. She thought it was just the dress rustling in the breeze before she saw Milly.

But Milly's expression looked different than normal, more pained. She didn't smile as she touched the green dress, or make to walk toward her as she normally did, to run her hand through Evelyn's bathwater. Instead, she turned on her heels and opened the door.

'Milly?'

But Milly was gone, the door partially open, the green dress hanging lopsidedly across the entrance.

Evelyn climbed out of the bath, pulling her clothes over her wet body. She hardly cared about drying herself, part of her already belonged to Milly's watery world. She retrieved the scalpel from the cold water and made her way to the door.

She could feel the cold weight of the green dress as she slipped past it. She looked out in the hallway and there, along the corridor, was a series of wet footprints.

Evelyn stepped through the water that puddled across the threshold, knowing that her watery footprints would now accompany those she was following. Trailing behind them, she made her way down into Wakewater's passageways, winding deeper into the main building until she passed through yet another door. The hallway behind it was narrower, perhaps indicating that she was in the servants' quarters, but it stopped suddenly at the summit of a staircase, leading downward to what she presumed would be a basement.

The footprints continued down the stairs. Evelyn made her way down after them, following not just the watery trail but the sound of voices rising up from below. As she reached the bottom, the sound became more audible – a repetitive, deep guttural exhalation – and alongside it, a higher-pitched trembling cry. It was a voice she recognised.

Pushing the door open, she knew what she would see.

There, lying in the water, two naked bodies clung together, moving as one. They were in a pool – a large tank, to be more precise, though the sides were hardly much higher than a bathtub and it was made of metal. She could see only part of Dr

Porter, his thigh muscles contracting and relaxing, not unlike the motion of a wave. But she could see all of his companion in front, moving in line with him but against the water that crashed against her breasts and stomach, a faint line of bruises across her throat like a necklace. He pushed against her back, forcing her lower in the water and then he seemed to shudder to a stop. Blanche, seeing that he was relenting, pushed herself back against him, riding the movement of the water until she shivered in a similar way.

The water was silent. Evelyn wanted to sink into the ground but she was rooted to the spot, scared to make a sound that might give her away.

Then Dr Porter stretched and waded toward the side of the tank. Climbing out, water drained from his body, a body covered in coarse dark hair, not at all like the surface of Blanche's smooth skin. She looked almost dry as she followed him out, her body seemed to repel the water.

'We'll resume your treatment tomorrow,' Dr Porter said, wrapping a towel around Blanche's shoulders.

She flashed him a smile, a secret teasing smile that Evelyn had thought was reserved just for her.

Evelyn felt numb as she stepped back into the shadows, as if her body had only just registered the impact of the cold water she'd been lying in earlier. She looked one last time at Blanche then retraced the watery footsteps back to the surface.

25

Kirsten

KIRSTEN SAT UP in bed. She touched her stomach, half expecting to feel her soft, fleshy insides hollowed-out like the women in her dream. But she was whole. She pulled the covers aside and Manon's notebook fell to the floor, the images and notes on drowned women scattering across the floorboards. She made her way to the window and pulled open the curtains.

Though it was still dark, Kirsten could see the river, dark and ominous, still in possession of that strange allure. What was it that attracted her? Was it the mysterious denizens it harboured? The ghosts of drowned women, calling her to join their number?

Kirsten moved away from the window towards the kitchen. She needed coffee and the clarity it would give her. But stepping into the hallway she was conscious of walking on water, and looking up saw the walls were running wet.

The walls, the ceiling, the floor all gushed water. It seeped through the plaster, like an open sore that refused to heal, water bubbling up from beneath the floorboards as it had in the cooling room.

'What do you want?' Kirsten screamed, falling down onto the soaked floor. It was as if she was enveloped in water that frustratingly never revealed its source. She touched the walls and the water ran down onto her arm. This was not a little water, the product of a faulty pipe somewhere. She could not rationalise it. Until some settlement had been reached, Wakewater would never be watertight.

Kirsten picked herself up off the floor, slung on her cardigan, and made her way towards the door. She could hear Sahara mewing behind her, perhaps trying to prevent her from going, though her efforts stopped at the threshold. She would not cross over into Wakewater's grounds and Kirsten could understand why. There were too many things here that couldn't be explained. As she made her way down the stairs, she wondered if she was being foolhardy, venturing out into its domain. But the water was already inside. What choice did she have?

The evening air was cold and Kirsten wrapped her cardigan tighter around her. She had not walked beside the river at nighttime. It was dark there, on the bridleway, away from the glow of streetlamps. But as her eyes became more accustomed, she could see that the river moved as it always did, no more menacingly than in the daytime. Perhaps it was because it always possessed a danger, irrespective of day or night. Kirsten had come to accept its perilous nature, now that she'd learnt so much about its past, about what it concealed within its waters.

She hadn't expected to see the woman with the long hair. She stood on the bank in the distance. Part of Kirsten had convinced herself that she had hallucinated the woman; that she'd materialised out of the stress of her break up, the anxiety of moving somewhere new. But here she stood, as real as could be. She was dressed in the same green dress, but it was faded now, torn and tattered from being in the water too long and, as

Kirsten approached, she saw that the woman had the same worn look in her countenance. Her hair ran wet across her shoulders.

Kirsten continued to move towards her, though all her instincts told her to run the other way. What had she read in Manon's notebook? That the rusalki lure you to the water, entangling you in their hair to drag you down beneath the surface. She could feel a cold spray from the water reach her skin. But she wasn't ready to belong to the water yet.

'Melusine?' she said when she was in speaking range.

She could see the woman more clearly now, could see that despite her decayed appearance, there was a vitality in her bearing. The water was energising her. She smiled at Kirsten and turning, raised her arm to the water.

And slowly, Kirsten saw a host of figures begin to emerge from the river. She saw their heads surfacing, their hair long and sleek and wet. Like a colony of seals nodding toward the bank, they regarding Kirsten. There were hundreds of them. These women in the water, existing just below the surface.

Kirsten looked back at Melusine. What did she want from her? There were enough of them, this aquatic army, to march out of the water and drag her back with them. There was no one else at Wakewater. No one would know that she had been taken. Only Manon would suspect, and who would believe her ravings anyway?

She hadn't brought any kind of weapon, anything she could use to defend herself, and she cursed herself for being so thoughtless. Even Manon had had the foresight to pick up a stick; she could have used it now to force them back. *To push them back down.*

Kirsten reached into her pockets in the desperate hope there would be something there, even Manon's torch could have sufficed as a weapon, though she'd have to get very close to swing it. But there was nothing inside, except... her hands clasped the cold metal of the locket Lewis had given her.

Wakewater was a centre for healing. It brought everything to the surface. The noxious fluids, the pain. Was that what the river wanted: her pain, her suffering? It had been fed drowned girls for so long, perhaps it was hungry for more misery and despair. Kirsten fingered the locket. Her own sorrow had been sustained by the river; that's why she had come to Wakewater, she'd craved the calming waters, the meditative stillness so she could process her pain. But she hadn't let it go. Not really.

She pulled the chain from her pocket. Melusine bent her head in its direction. Kirsten had thought that she would always keep it, a reminder to herself be cautious, not to give her heart away too easily. To keep it locked tight, like the locket itself. But she saw now that holding on to it was a mistake. It was perhaps better not to keep a part of yourself locked away and guarded from others. It was better to be open.

She thought of the painting she'd seen in Manon's notebook. *Found Drowned.* The image of the fallen woman washed up by the river, perhaps driven to the water because of the illegitimate child she carried. Her secret that wouldn't stay hidden forever. In her hand was a keepsake or a memento, something from her lover, perhaps; a promise of his love, though he had probably deserted her. Perhaps it had been a locket. She hadn't let go of her pain, it was what she clung to; it would only be taken from her by prising it out of her cold, dead fingers.

Kirsten wanted no part of the same fate. She waved the locket back and forth, and through the pendulum motion she thought she saw Melusine lick her lips. Didn't various ancient cultures make gifts to the river? Strange offerings to appease their tumultuous nature? Manon had been wrong: it wasn't about pushing them down at all, it was about placating its hunger.

Kirsten threw the locket into the river and watched as the women sank beneath the surface to retrieve their prize. For now, it would keep the water at bay.

26

Evelyn

EVELYN WAITED IN the basement. She'd been there all morning, hunched beside the immersion tank, thinking things through. She had spent the time scratching *Melusine* into the metal surface with the scalpel. She wasn't sure when Dr Porter and Blanche would reappear, ready to resume their watery love-making, but she knew it wouldn't be long, and when they did, she was ready for them.

She would deal with Dr Porter first. It was a shame in a way; she'd grown fairly fond of him and had almost believed his avidness in the Water Cure. But he was governed by baser instincts, like power and lust. She'd assumed that the ostentation of the solarium and the cooling room were due to Dr Cardew, but now she realised that Dr Porter was the only one who possessed any vision. Wakewater's simple philosophy didn't sit well with progress and he wanted to be at the head of something great, like Neptune in the mosaic, holding his trident high, surrounded by a throng of beautiful half-drowned creatures.

As for lust, it seemed to be curse of every man. The Rescue Society would have no fallen women to rescue if men could only control what was between their legs. Evelyn had read in her father's medical journals that hysterectomies and clitoridectomies were often performed to cure women of the very condition Dr Porter had diagnosed Evelyn with. They were so ready with the scalpel, these medical men, to cut and slice, yet no one had thought that castration was the logical solution to venereal disease.

Evelyn touched the point of the blade and watched the blood beading at the tip of her finger. Men needed to be emasculated. Then there would be no lust, no disease, no need to go probing around inside women with cold steel. And there would be no pregnancy. Women would not be driven into the water by the bastard babes growing inside of them. Weighing them down like rocks on the riverbed.

But what of Blanche? What was Blanche's crime? She was an adulteress, that was true, but it was her husband she was pledged to, not Evelyn. And she had given her so many hints about her involvement with the doctor. How else could she have known so much about the other patients, about his obstetric equipment, the secret tank he kept hidden in the basement? Blanche couldn't keep secrets and a part of her had wanted to tell Evelyn about it all, about what was really going on in the depths of Wakewater. Evelyn had let herself be deceived.

She heard footsteps on the stairs and returned to her hiding place in the corner of the room. She watched as they sauntered towards the tank, laughing boldly as they began to embrace, hungrily taking off each other's clothes. She watched Blanche's gown fall to the floor and saw her step, white and naked, into the water.

Evelyn knew she'd have to suffer their lovemaking again, but she couldn't reveal herself too soon, not until they were clinging to one another and dragging each other deeper into the water. Evelyn tried not to listen to Blanche's cries, the sound of the water crashing against the side of tank and spilling onto the floor.

She would know when the time was right, when they were too immersed in one other to notice anything else. Then she would creep towards the tank and sink into the water without so much as a splash, as Melusine would have done with her serpent tail. She would hurt them the way they had hurt her.

But it wasn't too late to walk away. She didn't have to follow this course. She could drop the scalpel and leave Wakewater behind her forever.

Dr Porter began to moan. From her hiding place she could only see his back, but she could see all of Blanche, her body leaning back in the water, lying there as if she was floating beneath Waterloo bridge with the rest of the sinners. She brought her body up, resting her head against Dr Porter's shoulder, panting feverishly into his ear.

She opened her eyes and they widened as she saw Evelyn.

But she didn't shrink away or call out, as Evelyn would have imagined. Instead, a smile spread across Blanche's lips. She wanted to be watched, to be caught. She clawed Dr Porter's back in delight. All the times she'd begged Evelyn to tell her about her work, about the fallen women Evelyn tried to reform, it was because she was one herself. The lowest kind of woman; one that dressed and acted the part of a lady, but really belonged at the very, very bottom.

Evelyn gripped the scalpel. She would wipe that smile from her lips even if she had to hold her beneath the water to do it. She ran toward the tank and plunged herself into the water in one swift motion. Her skirts billowed upwards and she welcomed the shock of the cold. The water was her element now.

Dr Porter turned at the sound of the splash, but Evelyn was too quick for him. She moved through the water with speed and sliced him across the stomach. One simple motion and the water began to turn red. Blanche screamed – a sound Evelyn imagined would have resembled the wailing of her dead child. Dr Porter staggered back and, clutching his abdomen, reeled towards her. But Evelyn raised the scalpel again and he backed away, falling into the side of the tank and pulling his weakened body out of the water. The exertion cost him: the skin stretched open as he hauled himself out, revealing a glimpse of his bloodied insides before he collapsed onto the floor.

'Help!' he called. 'Help!' Evelyn could hear him stumbling to his feet and then she saw him part-running, part-crawling towards the door. Wet and naked for all to see, trying to hold himself together as blood gushed from the slit Evelyn had made for him.

Blanche began to back away. Her rescuer, her dashing doctor, having abandoned her. She eyed the scalpel and held up her arms.

'Eve-' she managed to say before Evelyn grabbed her by the throat, holding her in the same way Milly had done, her fingertips finding the bruises that were already there. Evelyn pushed her beneath the water, forcing her low so she could repent. Water was the only path to redemption, that's what all those girls believed, as they threw themselves into the river; that despite the murk and the filth, it could wash away their sins. The only cure was by water.

Blanche had stopped trembling, her body inert. Only a few more seconds until she was pure again.

A hand reached into the water. The flesh was pallid, the skin broken. Evelyn looked up and there beside her was Milly. Her Melusine, offering her hand. Despite what the river had done to her – her face was worn, her green dress frayed and torn – she would always be her Milly. She smiled at Evelyn, and Evelyn took her hand.

Blanche resurfaced, spluttering against the side of the tank.

Milly led Evelyn out of the water. Holding hands, they crossed the room to the stairs. Two drenched girls, trailing water behind them. They wound their way up the staircase and along the corridor towards the main part of the house. Evelyn could hear voices in the distance, shouting in alarm, panic-stricken. It would not be long before they found her, before they would tear her away from Milly.

Milly didn't seem to notice. She walked unhurriedly, guiding Evelyn past the dining room, then the cooling room, with Neptune and his nereids watching them go. Then towards the solarium, with the large windows filled with nothing but the river. Milly opened one of the glass doors and suddenly they were outside, the warm air on their faces, the river just beneath them.

From this height you could see the vastness of the river's dominion. It coiled and arched its way towards the horizon. All waters eventually merge; they belong to larger bodies of water that seep out from deep within the earth. Primordial and everlasting, inherently female.

Milly helped Evelyn up onto the balcony railing. The river rushed beneath, dark and tumultuous. She could feel the air sweeping upwards, the spray from the water covering her face and neck. Her skirt billowed outwards, the heel of her shoe catching against the railing, which seemed to be the only thing preventing her from falling. That, and Milly. And then Milly was beside her, with the strange agility gifted to spectres. Holding hands, on equal footing, they looked over the precipice.

They would only have this one moment, this one secret moment, before the world was at the door, breaking it down. And then the doctors would be there and the treatments would begin all over again. Different treatments this time, for perhaps Evelyn was sicker than they realised. Sicker than *she* realised. It was not what Evelyn wanted, to be examined and prodded, denied books and ideas, to float unresponsively through the rest of her life. Besides, she was ready to uncoil her tail so that she could join Melusine in the river, ready to join that elemental sisterhood that existed just below the surface.

It was not so far down and she had Milly at her side. And Milly had done it before, after all. It was just a little fall.

'Evelyn!' she heard at her back, from across the solarium. A man's voice. Dr Cardew. Wanting to stop her, to cure her. 'Wait—'

But Evelyn let go.

27

Kirsten

KIRSTEN AND MANON walked beside the river. They moved slowly, Manon with the aid of a walking stick. It struck Kirsten as ironic that a walking stick would replace the one she habitually plucked from the bank, to drive the spirits of the river back down below. There was no need for that now. The river appeared sated. The waters were calm.

'It can't be a bad way to go,' Manon said, stopping to regard the river. 'To belong to that watery world.'

Kirsten nodded. She'd told Manon what she'd seen that night, the hordes of women emerging from the black waters. Not just the one or two Manon had glimpsed in her time as guardian at Wakewater. There was a whole underworld of women out there, floating just below the surface.

Manon clutched her hip, a flash of pain across her face.

'Are you OK?'

'I'm fine, dear.' She resumed walking. 'It hurts more the closer I am to the water.'

It was no wonder, Kirsten thought. The water had sought her out. It was in her body now, coursing its way through her veins.

'I find myself often thinking about something Virginia

Woolf said,' Manon continued, glancing up at the still waters. 'You know she walked out into the river? Filled her pockets with stones?'

Kirsten nodded again. Manon had told her before how she'd written her suicide notes before making her way to the water. Her actions so methodical, so clear.

'She said that women need a room of their own, a space to think, to write. In her day that wasn't so easy to acquire. Freedom for oneself had to be negotiated.'

Kirsten thought of Manon's flat, the rooms overflowing with her thoughts and ideas. Manon certainly needed a lot more space to house her intellectual life.

'But lately I can't help but think that it isn't enough. A room, no matter how large, will never be big enough. A flat, a house, even a mansion like Wakewater, why, still not enough. We – us women – need something more. We need a larger space. A river, a sea, an ocean. To counter all those years, those centuries, of being so confined. Of being sealed in and locked away.'

She paused and faced the river. Dark shadows crossed the surface as a flock of birds flew overhead.

'Perhaps we should head back?' Kirsten said, resting her hand on Manon's arm.

'No, no, I want to look into the river one more time. I want to see the faces in the water.'

Kirsten helped her down the bank. Manon's walking stick struck the boggy ground tentatively before she put any weight on it. Kirsten could understand Manon's need to look into the water. She understood its strange lure. She'd felt it herself. Many times. It was the river's curious pull that had brought her to Wakewater in the first place. And it had driven her down to the water's edge many times since, to deposit her keepsakes and mementos on the bank. There she'd watch the water women crawl out of the river to snatch up her offerings. Though she knew deep down that what she gave them was never quite enough to truly satisfy. The water always craved more.

But there had been some satisfaction for her in this simple act of giving. It felt good to leave her pain at the water's edge. She felt purged as it was washed away, taken up by those denizens of the deep. And she found her life at Wakewater strangely content, knowing the river depended on her. She was its guardian, until Manon had come back. Perhaps they would share this responsibility together.

Manon edged closer to the water. The ground was slipperier here, though the bracken and brambles provided some stability. Manon should have waited until she was completely healed, her walking stick made progress difficult; it slid about in the mud, struggling to gain purchase. It was hardly surprising that she fell, the stick swept out from under her as she crashed heavily to the ground.

'Manon!' Kirsten cried, negotiating the muddy bank in an effort to reach her.

'I'm fine,' Manon said with embarrassment. 'Get me up, get me up.'

It was as Kirsten began to lift her that she noticed the pale hand reach out of the water. The cold, dead fingers coiling around Manon's ankle.

'Kirsten!'

But Kirsten couldn't move. She was used to bringing the river gifts now. Of watching the water women claim their prize. They clearly mistook Manon for such a gift.

Manon squirmed against the river's grasp, her hands searching for her walking stick, which was just out of reach, half in the water. She looked toward Kirsten, imploring her to pick up her stick, 'Push her back down,' she hissed, 'push her back down!'

But Kirsten saw that it would do no good. Manon was already touched by the water. The river had already tried to claim her once

And she watched as a host of women began to emerge from the dark waters. Their hair wet shrouds across their faces.

'Kirsten?' Manon called again.

Kirsten was jolted into action. She gripped Manon under the arms and attempted to lift. She tried not to look at the river, at the women rising from the depths. She knew there would be a lot of them, expecting an offering. She didn't want to deny them, realising as she held Manon how insubstantial her other gifts had been. The locket and her keepsakes were only a foretaste. The river had a deeper hunger; it craved something bigger. Not just a portion of her pain. Something whole.

Kirsten could feel the river pull against her. It wanted Manon. She redoubled her efforts as if participating in some strange tug of war.

You pick up your sisters when they fall. And for a moment, looking out at the women rising, mist-like from the water, Kirsten imagined what their lives would have been like if someone had stopped them from falling. Perhaps in a different world, in a different time, they would have led good, full lives. She'd read in Manon's notebook that the police had once guarded Waterloo Bridge in an attempt to prevent prostitutes leaping to their deaths. But these women were already fallen in the eyes of society and there was no place else for them to go.

The river was their only course, their only way out.

But what a world these women belonged to now, this eternal female underworld. And it was a necessary world, even today. There must always be a space for the desperate and the fallen. Even if that meant the need to sustain it, to feed it from time to time.

Kirsten clutched Manon tightly by the shoulders. Hadn't she said herself how wonderful it would be to belong to such a world? Maybe all anyone needs is a little push.

Kirsten felt the river loosen its grip and suddenly in front of them stood the woman with the long, wet hair. She opened her pale arms. Kirsten could feel Manon's heart racing wildly.

It was only a little fall and Melusine was there to catch her.

Kirsten let go.

Acknowledgements

THE WELLCOME LIBRARY'S extensive catalogue was invaluable in researching the Water Cure and nineteenth century ideas and practices associated with women's health. Thanks are also due to my dear friend, Dr Tom Stammers for his historical guidance, to my agent, Johnny Mains, and Jen Hamilton-Emery for her editorial support. I am also indebted to the Saari Residence in Finland, maintained by the Kone Foundation, which provided serene and watery surroundings to finish the manuscript.